Ju

Elyse,

Congratulations,
You have manuverd
book one successfully
and I hope you
are hooked on
this series!

Best Wishes,
Carol

Mist of the Moment

The **“Season Series”** Novels

A Different Season

Fall of 2016

Mist of the Moment

Fall of 2017

Sweet Summer Rain

Fall of 2018

Wind of Change

Fall of 2019

Mist of the Moment

Carol Nichols

MIST OF THE MOMENT

 This novel is a work of fiction.

A Different Season

Mist of the Moment

Sweet Summer Rain

Wind of Change

Nichols Now books may be ordered at Amazon.com or contacting:

Nichols Now Publishing at

CarolNicholsAuthor@outlook.com

Or

www.adifferentseason.com

Cover photograph courtesy: Richard Fogg

ISBN-13: 978-0692985984

To Glen, my co-author
Thank you for your radiant spirit
And each moment of
Life we share!

To my first born, Pamela Carol an
Apology for omitting you in
A Different Season.
These books wouldn't be
Possible without your inspiration
As I live vicariously through you.

To my baby, Christopher Glen
For being a continual source
Of joy and encouragement.

To each reader, thank you for
Your continuing support

Please consider being an eye,
Tissue and organ donor.

ACKNOWLEDGMENTS

With much appreciation and thanks to…

My sister, Janice Southwick, for always believing in me and being the first to read each manuscript. I love you!

Eilene Gibbens, one of my closest friends, who has spent endless hours editing. It will take more than a hug to express my gratitude. Rest up, there is a book three to be read.

Linda Atkinson, for inviting me to your Thursday group that led me down this road.

Sue Pennington, Director of Bereavement, Russell-Murray Hospice, for pressing me to write through my grief and showing me I could find release through journaling.

Andrea Foster, editor/author, I applaud you for your vibrant personality, wise direction, and well-placed belief in Creative Quills writing group. You generously give to each of us your knowledge in editing, publishing, and writing. We are blessed you left life in the big city and with us now dwell.

First Christian Church, El Reno, many ideas have been gleaned within your walls.

My Praise and Prayer Group, thank you for your encouragement, friendship, compassion and tender conversations.

Brett Johnson, my grandson, for wrapping up the final product.

Richard Fogg, for your artistic gift of photography shown through the beautiful book cover. I know you were represented virtually in the first novel but now figuratively in this novel. Thank you for continuing this journey and being my friend.

Forward by
My Daughter
Pamela Nichols-Dinwiddie

Life is about moments. Moments that you spend with someone, moments you spend in prayer, moments in laughter, moments spending time outdoors, moments with those you hold dear. Moments are precious, and you should give your all.

A moment can last a second when you glance at someone and smile or moments can last forever. Whatever you do, just ENJOY your moments!

Love you all!

Pam

CONSTANCE LOUISE SINCLAIR

"JJ, I can't tell you how excited I am that you were able to locate the wild Mustangs because I am ready to ride," states Connie. "Are any of them at a point where we can start working with them?"

"I haven't decided," admits JJ as he pushes back from the table. "Great meal, ladies."

Connie's mind flows, *I miss riding Magic, but since he has been winning all his races, it isn't logical to take him out for any leisure riding.*

"I want to help," exclaims Amanda. "I just want to love all over any of them that show the slightest sign of being broke."

JJ continues, "The only thing we can do for the moment is to be in the pasture with them, let them become accustomed to us, and watch the pregnant mares. Our best chance is with the mares, and after they foal, of course, the babies will be easy to gentle."

"We can take oats out and see if we can get any broke to the bucket, then a halter. I don't like the fast break method, but would prefer to gentle them in, first with the saddle blanket, then saddle until they are comfortable," Doug advises.

Connie thinks, *"Good point, Doug. But what else would I expect because as Magic's trainer you have brought him from colt into the winner's circle."*

Amanda replies as she gently touches Doug's arm, "I'm ready."

"I know, it's been a long dry spell around here without any horses, but that's all changed. We need to get a few more cowboys to help with the wrangling, but we have plenty of saddles and tack," offers JJ.

Connie looks around the table as her heart softens at Amanda's and Doug's growing relationship and feels thankful for each person. Yes, the journey has been rocky, but now she feels the pure sense of gratitude for God's grace, mercy, and peace.

JEREMIAH JASON PAIGE

"Connie, if the rain lets up, would you consider going out with me? We haven't been anywhere together since your return from Oklahoma. We could have dinner and maybe dance for a while and talk."

"That would be fun," she answers while sitting on the settee in the sunroom. "We have only danced that one time in Oklahoma City, and it was a tiny floor."

JJ, chuckling, defends, "the small floor was to my advantage."

Connie smiles as she rolls her eyes and then decides, "Let's go even if the rain continues. I love driving in the rain as long as it's not torrential. There is just something about a gentle rain that seems relaxing," as Connie seems almost lulled by the soft sound from outside.

JJ questioned, "What were you thinking on your rental car? It probably could go back if you have decided to stay a while."

"JJ, you do realize, I will have to return to Oklahoma as I can't leave the estate just setting, not to mention the Wilson's are probably wondering how long I am going to impose on their kindness."

"You said you hadn't started getting it back up and running, didn't you?"

"Yes, but, thank you, Lord, the wells are coming back a little, as oil is at $50 a barrel, and the price should continue to climb. The house is close to being refurbished with many of the original pieces being made available from the buyers at the auction. I have some wonderful friends that truly looked out for my well-being. It was just such a harrowing time having to deal with the murder of the poor Walters woman, Charles' death from the fall, and Rosie and I locked up as material witnesses. I am so thankful all of that is in the past."

JJ, moving from the armchair to the settee beside Connie asserts, "I can't tell you how utterly and completely sorry I am for leaving you like that," as he softly touches her hand. "You and Rosie both."

She raises her face to meet his gaze, and those sad green eyes immediately turn to sparkles as she decries, "JJ, let's not go there, again. I am a stronger person and more in control of my life because of what has taken place. I so much want to be in this moment and all the moments ahead that, God in his mercy, has given us."

DOUGLAS HARTLY

"Amanda, I'm going to check on Magic and make sure Miguel is back and has given him water and feed," Doug states while he walks out of the living room into the kitchen and sees her at the sunroom door.

She glances his way and softly whispers, while she nods toward the sunroom, "I'll come with you, because I think JJ and Connie could use some time alone."

"Why do you think that?"

"They haven't been together in months, and before that, it was all haphazard during the murder investigation. I hope this is an indication of Connie's willingness to forgive and maybe renew some feelings between them. I realize the hardest part was him leaving while knowing she was sitting in jail."

"How did you get so perceptive? You certainly weren't feeling that melancholy towards me during these last few weeks while Connie was here, JJ gone and, just me and Magic, all alone in the stables. We haven't had any alone time, either."

"Well, keep talking, and I just might stay and clean the kitchen," she states while elbowing him.

"Come on, grab that umbrella, and let's make a run for it."

CONSTANCE LOUISE SINCLAIR

"Let's ask the kids to go with us this evening. I know Doug isn't familiar with the area, and I doubt Amanda will think to suggest anything. It will be fun. Is that okay with you?"

"I don't see why not," JJ replies but actually thinks, S*o much for alone time.*

"Great, this will be fun," Connie states as a clap of thunder followed by lightning illuminates the room, and she chills slightly.

Connie thinks, *Only a short time ago, lightning was a warning mechanism not to be overlooked for there were consequences, not only for me, but for ones I hold dear. Maybe the restlessness of my mind has been placed behind me. Has it, Lord? I have let my heart soften toward JJ, and I think I can let his past betrayal be forgotten.*

DOUGLAS HARTLY

"Connie, no! We can't all fit in your rental car."

JJ chides, "I'm with Doug, we'll help you all in the dually."

Connie frowns, "Okay, let's go while there is a lull in the rain."

As the girls wait for their doors to be opened, they quickly exchange glances and Connie and Amanda each swell with pride. The guys have on, not only boots but also hats, and look very impressive.

They head for the interstate, and Connie agrees, "There is no way we could have all fit in the rental, especially with those hats."

JJ jokes, "Yup, hats are important, especially if you are boot scooting to Brooks and Dunn."

Connie, as she speaks to everyone, enlightens, "You do know Ronnie Dunn moved to Tulsa after being forced to choose between the Christian College he was attending and his music career?"

Doug chuckles, "Connie, if we are going to play Oklahoma trivia, you do understand that we will be the only winners."

"I'm just trying to bring some Oklahoma knowledge to our friends. I don't know about you, Doug, but I do have some ties to Cali. Charles was born in Bakersfield."

JJ now jumps in, “My turn. Bakersfield, home of Dwight Yoakum, Buck Owens, Tanya Tucker and Merle Haggard.”

Connie turns in her seat and looks back at Doug, while she thinks, *How sweet, Doug has his arm around Amanda.* This pleases Connie as she manages to add, “Doug, it’s your turn to take up the Okies banner. Who else?”

“Well, Carrie Underwood, Blake Shelton, Toby Keith and the great, Garth Brooks.”

As their attention turns to Amanda who has a smile on her face but quickly turns to a questioning look, admits "What? That's not fair! JJ named all I can think of."

Everyone, almost in unison agrees, “Come on!”

"Okay, okay, if I'm forced to participate," Amanda questions, "Do you know who wrote our state song?" Giving them a little time to ponder before she continues, "I didn't think you would. California's state song was written by Frankenstein."

This revelation meets with complete silence, and then everyone breaks into laughter as Doug chides, “Very appropriate, thunder, lightning, rain, and Frankenstein. Oh, my!"

Connie, brought back to the moment by Doug’s proclamation along with a clap of thunder, blurts, “JJ, you pick some place to stop. We don’t have to go much farther, Doug is right, it is pouring."

JJ agrees, “Great,” as he maneuvers a swift right into O’Brien’s Pub, making everyone scramble to maintain their balance.

JEREMIAH JASON PAIGE

As they sit, safely, in the parking lot, they all lean forward, look up at the sign, and Connie exclaims, "Yea, O'Brien's Irish Pub," with an emphasis on Irish. "I might meet some of my relatives in here."

Entering the establishment, Doug holds the first door for the girls and JJ, then JJ reciprocates and holds the next door, while the ladies enter along with Doug. But Doug's stay is brief, as JJ is quickly met by Doug's resistance when Doug backs into JJ in full retreat from O'Brien's.

JJ lets the door close, thus leaving the girls inside locating their ID's. "Whoa buddy, what's the problem, you do know how to dance, don't you?"

Doug begins his explanation, "Yes, but…," before he can continue, the door opens, and the girls, in complete excitement, exclaim, "This is going to be sooooooo much fun. Come on!!"

AMANDA BORDILLON

"I have never done this. I'm so excited! Hurry, let's go!"

Doug shakes his head in despair, he feels like a trapped animal as he sees JJ's forlorn, helpless stare. They advance toward the front, each with their respective date, then the DJ hands them a microphone and discloses, "Hello, folks. Welcome to Karaoke Night!"

DOUGLAS HARTLY

Doug takes the ladies' drink orders, and briskly pushes JJ ahead of him to the bar area. "What are you thinking? Get us out of here!"

JJ, as he looks back toward their table, sees the big smile on Amanda's face and immediately softens, as he knows he cannot drag his niece, let alone, Connie, back into the rain.

"Doug, ole boy, welcome to the wonderful world of love and the price each of us pays to enjoy it. This is how the love-game works. You do things that make them happy. In return, you spare yourself countless hours of pure agony where your only refuge is in the barn with Magic."

Doug now shakes his head in disbelief, as he tells the bartender, "Make mine a double!"

CONSTANCE LOUISE SINCLAIR

Amanda, grabbing Doug's hand, motions to JJ and Connie to come join them, but Connie, in a loud voice directs, "You kids, go on. JJ and I will sit this one out." Turning her attention to JJ, she states, "How fun is this?"

JJ, with a big smile, agrees, "I know it is wonderful seeing Amanda having such a good time." While, also thinking, *"I'm going to be dog meat before this is all over by the look on Doug's face."*

As Connie and JJ watch the others, Connie, with a serious look, admits, "JJ, you're right. I'll turn in the rental car. I would like to see Bakersfield again. I've only been there once, and that was after Charles and I had spent a couple of weeks in Vegas. Charles wanted to drive through the area and at least know he had been in the town of his birth. He was three months when they left for Oklahoma."

JJ agrees, "I think that would be the best thing. No reason to pay for the time you aren't driving the car."

DOUGLAS HARTLY

Doug glances out the kitchen window of the RV looking for some sign of movement in the house. He thought JJ would be up by this time of the morning. *I might go on up to the house and wait in the sunroom or even knock on JJ's bedroom door as he sleeps downstairs.* Doug could hardly wait to give JJ grief about last night. Connie and JJ only participated that first time, and the rest of the evening it was him and Amanda. Every time they made it back to the table, he became more riled, as JJ and Connie were deep in conversation, while he was handed that mic once again.

From the beginning, he had opted to stay in the RV instead of staying at the house. Where had the time gone? Has it been over a year since he and Magic came to the Bordillon Ranch?

Doug stands, poised with his coffee cup, still looking toward the house, but no longer seeing anything as he remembers the first time he realized he had feelings for Amanda. Yes, Doug thinks, *He exits the tack room, he stops to observe Amanda at Magic's stall as she strokes Magic's neck and Magic nuzzles her. Amanda's long shiny ebony hair almost disappears against the black of Magic's coat. As his gaze continues down, he gives a quick smile as he notices her boots and the missing flip flops she wore the night they first met. Advancing his gaze back up, he is drawn to the ribbons hanging loosely in her left hand, the color of her blue shirt. His eyes linger for only a mere moment at her tiny belted waist when he realizes she was very pleasant to look upon as his heart, ever so softly, skips a beat.*

With a crisp nod, Doug places his cup in the sink and leaves for the stable as he is firmly in agreement with JJ. The price you pay for love is small, very small, indeed!

CONSTANCE LOUISE SINCLAIR

Connie, rolling over, glances at the phone that lies vibrating on the nightstand. She recognizes the number and stiffens herself in response to her feelings of procrastination. Connie thinks, *I have just decided to remain in Cali. Lord, wasn't that where You were telling me to settle, at least for a while, and attempt to understand my feelings for JJ? Yes, Lord, how can I possibly live two lives?*

Charles found a life out here, whether right or wrong. Doug and Magic are also here and, if what I see when Amanda and Doug are together, will be for a long time to come.

JJ has procured the beautiful Mustangs from the Bureau of Land Management that we all can hardly wait to start working so we can have a few pleasure horses to ride.

Amanda and I seem to be in a place where we each can speak of Charles, as my husband and also her father, without feeling uncomfortable.

If I stay, I might be able to tell her of some of the Sinclair traditions and she can, in return, talk about her mother and her heritage on that side. I know nothing of her mother. Are there other siblings besides JJ?

Okay, Lord, if I am supposed to stay, you're going to have to help me figure this out before I make this return call to Oklahoma.

AMANDA BORDILLON

Amanda looks in the refrigerator and asks, “Somebody call Doug and see if he has eaten breakfast? Hello, you two, anybody awake? ”

Amanda turns and sees JJ looking at his phone but making no attempt to call. JJ shakes his head and with a chuckle thinks, *I dread seeing Doug, but then, if I can get Doug with the girls, he won't be able to yell about last night.* As he lifts his phone, Amanda blurts, "Never mind, I’ll go get him."

JJ looks to Connie and notices she is oblivious to anything going on around her as he gently cups her hand in his. "What is it, Babe?"

Connie takes a deep breath and confesses, “Oh, J, I’ve set something in motion, and I wish I hadn’t.”

JJ stiffens as he inquires, “What might that be?” thinking the worst.

"I've just spoken this morning with the company that has built the prototype for Charles' Evaporative system. When I negotiated the terms, oh JJ, it was months ago, and I…"

JJ rapidly blinks as he becomes concerned and asks, “Connie, if you are serious about staying and letting us have a chance to rekindle what we had before, will you let me try and help? You don’t have to handle things on your own any longer. Can we, maybe slowly, but can we lean towards being partners? I’m not talking only about business partners, but partners in everything.”

“That sounds so simple, but…”

“But what?”

“It’s an agreement I made with the France implement company. JJ, I didn’t want to let the law firm handle this. I was trying to save money and be more assertive, and in control, so I negotiated the conditions of the agreement myself. It was my idea to use our oil sites as the test location for the prototype. I told them I wanted to be involved in all aspects and would make myself available. I just wanted something, anything that would consume me to the point I could fall into bed at night and sleep. I wanted something to keep my mind worn to the point of exhaustion, so sleep would not evade me night upon night."

“What are you telling me, Connie?”

"I'm trying to tell you, I'm contractually obligated to have the estate and well sites open and available upon their request. I've put them off during my initial visit with Amanda as I felt, at that time in our relationship, I just couldn't leave. I also assured them I would expeditiously review all paperwork."

“Okay, how long?”

“They have given me two days. I need to leave tomorrow,” Connie states.

Connie, touched by this concern, feels the warmth from his hands engulf her and closes her eyes as she thanks God, thinking this is His answer.

DOUGLAS HARTLY

"Wonderful breakfast...a...lunch. Well, it was still morning, technically, when we started. Thanks for including me. What was the name of the biscuits we had?"

"7UP."

"Hope we have them every time, but everything was good," Doug adds as he realizes that he and Amanda are carrying most of the conversation during the meal.

Doug stands and states, "Well, thanks again." Doug turns his attention to JJ, and asks, "Could I speak with you when you get the opportunity?"

JJ cringes as he thinks he might as well get this over, and chokes, "Sure, I'll walk back to the stables with you."

A few feet from the house, JJ begins, "I'm sorry about last night. I just couldn't bring myself to cut short the evening as Amanda seemed to be having a good time. Doug, you were a true gentleman for hanging in there as you did."

"I'm over all that, but if you had been up before I had coffee this morning, I'm not sure I would have made the same statement at that time."

JJ eases his stance and sighs, "Well, that certainly makes me feel better. What did you want, then?"

"I am worried about you and Connie. You're not on the outs again, are you? You two looked so pensive at the table. When I asked Amanda at the sink, she said everything seemed okay when she left to get me. What's up?"

"Doug, Connie has some pressing business obligations, and if we are not able to find a solution, she will have to leave for Oklahoma tomorrow, at the latest."

“Is there anything I can do?” Doug inquires.

"I wish there were. I've got part of it handled as to the paperwork that needs to be reviewed and signed. That can be managed electronically, but Connie has obligated herself to have the estate and adjoining lands available upon the implement companies’ bidding. She feels as if she has overly intruded on the Wilson's hospitality and doesn't feel comfortable about imposing on them any further."

“JJ, that’s a big one. Who could you possibly trust with all that?”

JJ paces and grumbles, "Think, Doug, you lived there on the estate. There has to be someone. I honestly need her to stay. We are finally getting to a comfortable position in our relationship. But now, this surely can‘t be good."

“I don’t know, JJ. The last time I was there was for the wedding and…”

JJ spins on his heels toward Doug and sputters, “Doug, you’re a genius. I could kiss you!" JJ has both hands on Doug’s shoulders, shakes him vigorously and just stops short of the promised kiss.

JEREMIAH JASON PAIGE

JJ, like a speed racer, makes it to the house in record time. He slings the sunroom door open, he hollers, "Connie, Connie, where are you?"

Amanda, startled, jumps up, "JJ, what's wrong?"

"Where's Connie, where is she?"

Amanda, unable to get her wits about her, points to the stairs.

JJ, taking the stairs two and three at a time, gets to Connie's room just as she opens the door to see why all the loud voices.

JJ grabs her by both arms and laments, "I spoke with Doug, and he has the answer to keeping the developers happy and you at the ranch."

Connie walks back in her bedroom, obviously elated at this news. "That's wonderful. What's his idea?"

"He didn't say it exactly, but he did tell me the last time he was at the estate was the wedding, Rosie and Pete's wedding."

Connie slowly turns, affirms, "Why didn't I think of that? Rosie and Pete are perfect. They can house-sit! Rosie still isn't working, and it won't be that far for Pete to drive downtown to Police Headquarters. Oh JJ, let's call now. I can fax her a letter so she can act as my proxy."

ROSIE REDMOND ROSEMAN

"What do I have to do exactly?"

Connie realizes she has poured out this whole situation way too fast for Rosie to understand, takes a deep breath and begins again. "Rosie, you remember Charles' Evaporative System, right?"

"Yes, the plans on the flash drive that Louis Ludlow stole the day he pushed Charles down the stairs at the estate," Rosie answers.

Connie continues, "Okay. The courts have ruled that Charles' estate is the rightful owner and ordered the flash drive containing the contents of Charles' computer and the schematics for the system returned to me. The French Implement company contacted me with an offer to develop the prototype, and in return, they wanted the option of all sales in the United States. I agreed, and then I made them an offer to test the prototypes on my wells while assuring them I would be available to participate in the initial startup. Oh Rosie, when I made this offer, I had nothing but time on my hands and was looking for any distraction that would keep my mind busy.

Rosie, JJ and I are on the brink of rediscovering what we had in Oklahoma and seeing if it is possibly real, but if I'm forced to return to Oklahoma…Rosie, it just wouldn't be conducive, to say the least, for our relationship.

I need someone to stay at the estate and be at the installers' beck and call to unlock the sites and keep the estate open, so they can utilize the barn area for the development."

“Connie that is just such a big ole place. I’d have to drive back and forth twice a day. What time would I have to be out there?”

“No, JJ and I thought you and Pete could just house-sit and then you wouldn’t have to drive. I can open a household account at MidFirst under your name, and you can use the debit card to pay for everything. As for the keys, they are all labeled and in the key box in the kitchen office area. What are you thinking? Can you handle this? You're not working, are you?"

"Let me run this by Pete and see if it is mandatory that he live within the Oklahoma City city limits, since his employer is the Oklahoma City Police Department. It will add to his drive, also. How soon do you have to know?"

“If you are unable to do this, I need to be on a plane tomorrow at the latest.”

“I’ll call you back as soon as Pete gets home. Maybe 5 or 6. Will that be okay?”

“Rosie, certainly, I just am thankful that you are even considering helping. Talk with you later tonight. Hugs!”

CONSTANCE LOUISE SINCLAIR

Connie looks for JJ, sees the front door open and finds him pensive on the porch as he seems to be surveying his surroundings. “There you are.”

“Was it a yes?”

"She has to speak with Pete before making any decision, so it will be after he gets home from work."

JJ encircles her with a soft and all-encompassing hug as he groans, “I would think Pete would agree, don’t you?”

“That’s my prayer, JJ.”

“Then, that’s my prayer, also.”

Connie turns and begins to ask something of JJ, but then changes her mind and interjects, "Will you take me out to see the Mustangs?”

“Sure, let’s go.”

“Look at them,” Connie states. "Just look at them. You can hear the power and see the beauty of God's magnificent creatures so clearly when they are in motion."

Connie with a soft smile, turns and looks at JJ, and he immediately questions, "What? What is going on in that head of yours?"

"I just thought if Rosie and Pete are not able to stay, and I have to leave tomorrow, everything will be all right, now that I know."

JJ, taking her hand, “Know what?”

“What you said on the front porch as you held me.”

JJ looks perplexed. “I’m afraid I’m not following you. What exactly are you referring to?”

"When I said I was praying Rosie and Pete would stay at the estate, and you said, ‘that will be my prayer, also.’ Oh, JJ, that fills me with joy to hear you say you pray. I wanted to ask if you knew God because that is paramount to me. God is a fundamental part of my life, and I give everything to Him.”

“Okay.”

Connie continues, “You do believe in God?"

"Yes, I do. But I can't say I speak with Him often. I went to church a lot as a child, but I was drug unwillingly.

"Oh, my!"

"No, let me finish. Our mother, Margaret's and my mother, was devout and she drug us kids to church every time the doors were open, which was three times a week, if not more. When I was old enough to make my own decisions, I quickly backed off to just Sunday mornings. Then that became hit and miss, and pretty soon it was just miss, so God and I know each other, but not like we should."

Connie discloses as she turns into him, “I’m still okay with that for we all live under God’s grace.”

ROSIE REDMOND ROSEMAN

"Hello, honey. Pete gave it a thumbs up, so we are all set. I need through the weekend to get things together."

"Rosie, you have no idea how much I appreciate you doing this for JJ and me," answers Connie. "I will get in touch with Geri Wilson. She's the neighbor the first section north of the estate, and let her know that you will be house sitting for me."

"Okay, great."

CONSTANCE LOUISE SINCLAIR

Connie gleefully enters the kitchen to find JJ, Doug, and Amanda at the large circular table, deep in conversation. She stops a moment to let the conversation complete and as they look her way, proclaims, "Rosie and Pete are in agreement and will be at the estate next Monday."

JJ rises as Doug and Amanda both state, "That's perfect."

Connie looks Amanda's way and asks, "Amanda, hope you can put up with me a little while longer!"

Amanda, with a smile, offers, "As if you have to ask."

As JJ shows his pleasure and hugs Connie, she hears thunder in the distance and suddenly feels the uneasy warning she thought was no longer a part of her life. "Oh Lord!"

JEREMIAH JASON PAIGE

JJ exits into the sunroom and glances at the clouds as he states, "Steaks on the grill are in order for this evening if the weather holds off."

Amanda jumps up and agrees, “I’ll get them out of the freezer. Ribeye good? Connie, will you wrap some potatoes and pop them in the oven, and Doug, see if we have everything for a salad."

Connie, as she oils a potato, thinks as she hears the thunder again along with the feeling of foreboding, *Lord, what is all this? You made the way clear for Rosie and Pete to stay at the estate. Why am I feeling these feelings again?*

CONSTANCE LOUISE SINCLAIR

"I have faxed the proxy letter to Pete at work for Rosie to use at the estate and I set up the account at MidFirst Bank for her use, also."

"What about the Wilson's?" JJ asked.

"I've tried them. That is the only thing left. I certainly need to speak with Geri to let her know what's going on. I don't want her getting concerned and going down there when there is no reason. But no answer for now. Maybe later."

"Do you have her cell number, or his?"

"Yes, I do. I never call Geri's cell as I don't know if she even carries it. They are always at the farm as they have livestock and even have a phone in the barn, so I just call the house number. I'll try again later."

DOUGLAS HARTLY

Doug enters through the sunroom brusquely, stops and states, “I’ve placed Magic in several upcoming races, and the final is at Santa Anita. Who’s up for a road trip?”

"I can hardly wait. Do you realize how long it's been since I’ve been at the track with Magic?" states Connie. "It seems an eternity, and now I have someone to root with on the sidelines.”

Amanda chimes in, "What fun, and just think, an easy decision about placing our bet."

JEREMIAH JASON PAIGE

"I'm going! I can hardly wait to finally be hands-on along with Doug."

Amanda glances JJ's direction and looks a little apprehensive. "What about the Mustangs? There are several mares pregnant, and we aren't confident on their delivery dates. Miguel seems to think several will foal within the next few weeks, and we will be gone longer than that."

JJ attempts to reassure Amanda. "Yes, and Miguel, Jose, and Felipe are all capable of handling the situation. If I had the least bit trepidation about that, I would be the first to admit it."

Connie enters the room and joins the conversation. "JJ, you need to go. I'm certain Doug would appreciate your help, and you were part owner of Magic up until a few months ago." A sly smile comes to her lips at those words, remembering JJ had transferred the half ownership of Magic from himself to her as an attempt to cover what he deemed omissions on his part in their relationship, like leaving her and Rosie sitting in a jail cell while he took time to figure things out.

ROSIE REDMOND ROSEMAN

"Pete, what just happened? Pete, where are you?" Rosie runs down the grand staircase while she looks every direction from the vantage the stairs provide.

PETER ROSEMAN

"Yeah, Danny, I've called to ask…whoa, Danny, are you feeling that? It's another earthquake and a large one. I'll call you back. I hear Rosie hollering for me."

"Pete, there you are. I don't ever want to be on that stairway when that happens again. I felt it sway immediately after the boom hit. It must have been over a minute in duration."

Pete checks his phone. "Channel 9 just issued a 5.3 eight miles west of Pawnee at 7:44 and waiting for confirmation from USGS."

"I glanced at the clock, and it was 7:45 exactly when I first felt it, so it took a minute to get to us. I'm not sure I like this big ole place of Connie's if this is going to be happening," states Rosie as she securely latches her arms around Pete and takes refuge.

"We'll be okay. You're just used to our apartment. Remember we're doing this for Connie and JJ, and I kind of like staying exactly where we were married and entertained all our friends. You are happy Rosie, aren't you?"

"Yes, Pete, I'm still head over heels in love with our love, and the only regret I could have is not meeting you sooner. It doesn't get much better than this. Thank you, Lord!"

Little does Rosie dream that over the next few months her resilience to living at the estate will be put to the test about more than one thing!

AMANDA BORDILLON

“Another W in the win column. He’s just marvelous. Absolute splendor in motion.”

“Yes, he certainly is. These last months have put him to the test, and Magic has met and exceeded every one,” Doug replies.

“I’m happy we were all able to travel in the horse hauler. That makes it even more perfect, family and friends,” adds Amanda.

Connie can’t agree more as she listens to Amanda, but can’t help but wonder which column Amanda has placed her beneath, family or friend. Connie nods and thinks, *whichever it is, it doesn't matter as I’m happy to be included. Yes, it has been a rough road, but finally, a small respite has arrived! Thank you, Lord.*

“I’m glad this worked out because now you can see how lonely this circuit can be, but the last race was another win. So, we’re ready to roll,” states Doug. “I’ll leave Magic in the stable until we grab something to eat, then we can load him and hit the road.”

Doug looks toward Amanda while he simultaneously nods in Connie's direction. "Connie, are you okay? You seem a million miles away."

Connie straightens and relates, "I just remembered the last time I was here was when Louis Ludlow found Magic and figured out that Charles was my husband. That's how he located Charles in Oklahoma and pushed him to his death.”

Connie thinks, *its times like these that push the buttons that release the memories.* Connie felt the need to crumble, to crumble in a heap and cry.

At that moment, she felt Charles' presence, but in an unnerving way and not in the comforting manner of before. *Charles, our moments are never truly realized until they return to me as memories! What, Charles? What are you trying to tell me?*

JEREMIAH JASON PAIGE

"What sounds good? Let's get some food in you, and you'll feel better."

Connie nods an indistinguishable answer, as she closes her eyes and avoids any further conversation.

The trip back home seems arduous for all concerned, and any conversation is muffled and only from the front seat.

At the ranch, Magic is unloaded and secured in his stall as JJ looks to Connie and utters, "Connie, you've seemed so distant from the moment we left to eat. Are you all right?" he adds as he reaches for her hand. He feels no opposition as she gives a slight acceptance to his effort, but Connie knows, yes, she knows, she has to go back as her life still is not her own. The feeling for her need to flee is overwhelming.

CONSTANCE LOUISE SINCLAIR

Connie grasps her phone after finding a secluded place and tries to dismiss her negative thoughts before she puts it to her ear.

"Hello, Rosie. Oh, Rosie, good to hear your voice. I need to talk and in the worst way. I am so, so unnerved almost to the point of panic-stricken."

"Connie, okay, what's the matter? Is someone hurt?"

"No, I didn't mean to scare you. Oh Rosie, it's just, just…"

"Just what, Connie? Tell me. You're frightening me."

"It's just a disturbing feeling I received from Charles. I've never felt him like this."

"When, just now?"

"No, earlier today with JJ, Amanda, and Doug. We've been on the race circuit for a couple of months with Magic and just returned from Santa Anita, which was Magic's last race."

"So, Magic didn't do well?"

"No, he was wonderful as always. Makes my heart so happy when I get to be present at his races, but..."

"But what, Connie? When did it happen? When did you feel Charles?"

"Rosie, it was just a flashback moment as I stood where I had spoken with Louis Ludlow, and then I felt Charles' presence. I immediately had this uncontrollable urge to fall to pieces, and it was a struggle to control my emotions with everyone around."

"Honey, don't you think that is to be expected every now and again? Memories can just sneak up on you when you're not prepared."

"I don't know any longer, Rosie. It was Charles. The same as always. The same as I have felt him from the first moment he revealed himself to me in the kitchen as I stood reading the mail only weeks after his passing. I don't understand what he is trying to tell me, though, Rosie, it feels like a warning. Am I living in a pretend world? Oh, Rosie, where in life exactly do I belong?"

"I can't answer that, sweetheart. Tell me what you need. What can I do?

"I don't know what to do. Oh, Rosie!"

"Connie, I will help however I can and will continue to support you in any and everything you feel you need to do."

"I know. I need to cry. Rosie, I need a good cry but I can't. Not here. Not now. How can I explain my feelings to all of them when I don't know myself?"

"I can only surmise your feelings, where you are and the journey you are on. You know I love solving a good mystery, but Charles is way beyond me. If you were here, we both could have a good cry."

"You need to cry, too?"

"Yes, right now I do," confesses Rosie in a subdued tone.

"Well, I'm coming home!"

"Are you certain?"

"Yes, I knew it when all the memories came flooding back at the track with Magic. I just wanted to run and run and run, and the only place I know to run is home. I need to come home!"

"Well, that won't make me mad. I will welcome you with open arms and a big hug. I have become a little concerned but didn't want to make you feel as if you needed to return.

Connie asks, "About what?"

"Just stuff that has happened while staying here at the estate."

"Rosie, what's happened? Have I caused a rift in your marriage? Please tell me I haven't."

"No, no, ma'am, you certainly have not. We are still quite in the honeymoon phase of our marriage."

"Then, what's your concern?"

"Well, it's the earthquakes, or should I say the continuation of earthquakes. There has been one at Cushing. You remember sometime back the 5.8 quake in Pawnee?"

"Yes, I remember, and my heart goes out to that town and damages it suffered, but I thought it was just a 5."

"No, it has been upgraded to a 5.8, breaking the record of the 5.7 earthquake in the '50's at El Reno. Pawnee now holds that record."

"Rosie, so there have been more?"

"Yes, big ones."

Connie queries, "The same intensity?"

"Yes, a 5.7 in Prague and now a few days ago the 5.3 in Cushing, and they all were felt here at the estate. It was a little frightening and intimidating."

"Oh, I can only imagine, but Rosie, what is being said about the Cushing quake? You do realize Cushing is the largest oil storage facility in the world. What would happen if those tanks ruptured?"

"I don't even want to let my mind go there," Rosie continues. Things are getting a little tense. The injection wells are a hot topic, and some of your neighbors, at least I think they are your neighbors, are questioning the use of the prototype set up at your well sites. They have never seen anything in use like this, and I'm at a loss to quiet their concerns."

"Are you telling me you don't feel safe?"

"Oh, I have Pete at nights, and during the day, I keep the estate gates shut so anyone wanting entry has to use the intercom."

"So, you don't feel secure enough to leave them open? That helps with the main entrance on the west, but what are you doing about the north entry the scientists and technicians are using?"

"Nothing at the moment but from what Pete has been hearing, the populace of Southern Kansas has formed a coalition to force the Oklahoma Corporation Commission, the Oklahoma legislative body and the Governor into action as tolerance for the intensifying quakes has reached an end, at least to the oil deprived state to our north."

"Well, that's settled. Whatever apprehension I was feeling about staying in California has been validated. I'll be on a plane tomorrow."

AMANDA BORDILLON

Amanda, without a word, crosses the room, as she meets Connie at the sunroom door. "I was just coming to look for you. Are you okay? You were so quiet the entire drive."

"I know, I'm not feeling well. My head is pounding, and I just spoke with Rosie, and I need to go home. I'm checking into a flight for tomorrow."

Connie ascends the stairs as Amanda turns to look for JJ.

JEREMIAH JASON PAIGE

"Amanda, slow down. You think there must be problems in Oklahoma, and what was that last part?"

"Connie's checking into a flight home, tomorrow!"

"That was her exact words, 'a flight *home*'?"

"Yes."

"Okay, Amanda, Doug and I will be at the house in just a few."

Doug asks, "What's going on?"

"That was Amanda. Connie is checking into a flight to Oklahoma, immediately."

"What has happened?"

"She's not sure, but Connie used the word *home*, which tells me all of our plans have unraveled. I was under the impression that she has considered us her family and this her future home, not Oklahoma."

"Maybe you are jumping to conclusions," Doug remarks.

"Maybe so, but I had just convinced her to let me into her life to help with her problems. Doesn't sound like I was the first person she went to. No, didn't ask me to help figure this out."

CONSTANCE LOUISE SINCLAIR

With the bedroom door ajar, JJ enters, sees the partially filled suitcases, and items in her grasp. He shakes his head in disapproval, briefly clenches his fist, but remains silent.

Connie turns, and as their eyes meet, her posture straightens as she gains her full height and lets the blouse fall to the bed. With chin high, she bites her lower lip and her right eyebrow raises as she takes a deep breath.

JJ slowly shakes his head as he averts his eyes and strokes his hair in what seems a soothing gesture. He attempts to remain calm while he displays a false smile and forcefully closes the door.

Grabbing her shoulders, he utters, "Tell me!"

DOUGLAS HARTLY

Doug turns at the sound of the shutting door and sees Amanda with a fixed gaze at the base of the stairs.

He advances with palpable anticipation as they clasp hands.

Amanda breathlessly strokes her stomach to control the fluttering from within.

JEREMIAH JASON PAIGE

"JJ, there you are," Amanda exclaims with heart pounding while tingling all over. "Why aren't you answering your phone? Doug, I've found him."

Doug rushes towards Amanda's voice and confesses, "JJ, you had us worried. We were both so concerned. What happened?"

JJ rises, shakes his head repeatedly and with a glazed look stares at the floor and then gives an impromptu laugh and states, "I guess it's all appropriate. But it seems like payback for leaving her all those months in Oklahoma with not even a word. It was wrong, I knew it was wrong the whole time, but, you know what, Doug?" JJ reasons in an exaggerated laugh.

"What, JJ?"

"All those months seems to have given her resolve. A determination to tackle life on her own, because she had this calm resignation about her that I haven't seen before."

"Okay, are you telling us there is a misunderstanding, and she just is leaving to give you both some space or is she…"

"No, Doug," JJ continues with some false enthusiasm. "Connie's still disconcerted from being at the track. I can't get through to her. I just want her to let me help. She seems to jump from calm resolve to a quivering mass of doubt."

"Doubt about what?"

"I don't know. Doubt about us? Doubt about being here? Doubt of the unknown? She kept repeating, 'I don't know what to think. I can't figure it out.' "

"Did you try and tell her that a few more days wouldn't hurt anything?"

"No, I was too blown away over her last statement."

"JJ, did I miss something? What statement was that?" Doug asks as he clears his throat and glances at Amanda to see if she has noticed the tonal change in her uncle's voice and the gaunt look that has overtaken him.

"I told Connie I'd go with her and help get everything settled. That's when I noticed her eyes."

Amanda in a fearful tone, offers, "What about her eyes?"

"Connie's eyes were distant…" JJ takes a long measured breath. "They weren't those soft green eyes that so eagerly calls me to protect and safe guard.

Doug, that's when I thought that it is déjà vu, and maybe it's better to let life, our lives, rearrange some. But now I don't know which is better. She has been different from the moment we noticed her during the flashback at the track as she relived her encounter with Ludlow and felt Charles' presence.

And, in her room, she took a step back and said, 'I'm going *home*!' It was so final. Then this unnatural stillness came over her.

How do you fight that, Doug? How do you fight something like that?"

CONSTANCE LOUISE SINCLAIR

Connie sits in one of the many chairs she has maneuvered and lets a slow breath escape. She rubs her hands together, glimpses at a clock in the airport terminal and reaches for her phone.

"Rosie, I have a couple of hours before I board, but I just checked the screen, and it shows my flight is on time, so I'll land around 7:30. What do you mean, something has happened?"

"I didn't tell you last night, because I didn't know. When Pete got in from work, after we spoke, I said you were coming home. He said he didn't want to tell me about what he knew as he didn't want me scared, so Pete just told me to keep the alarm system on at all times and doors locked unless he was here. I thought he was just over apprehensive about the questioning neighbors, but last night upon hearing you had decided to come home, he told me."

"Told you what, Rosie?"

"Pete had returned home early last week and upon entering from the back immediately noticed dirt inside the door in the walkway. He entered the kitchen to look at the note pad we use to tell each other where-the-heck we are or aren't in this big ole place and it wasn't on the end of the bar. He walked to the desk, a drawer was partially open, the note pad was on the desk, and the pages were ruffled as if someone had rifled through it. He walked the rest of the house, then checked out back and the stables, but found nothing."

"So, Pete thinks what, Rosie? Happenstance or someone had been there?"

"He's leaning toward the latter as the cameras caught someone. He didn't tell me except to keep locked up all the time instead of nights only, but since you are coming, he wanted you to think on your way if anything could have sparked this?"

"Rosie, are you okay?"

"I was, but now with the shooting, I'm a little on overload. Oh, Connie, I had just let my mind rest. I was trying to be like you and be just in this moment, to slow down and give life a chance to be embraced and listen to the simple hum of the day. Isn't that what you told me, we only have this moment? It doesn't matter whether we stand in the sunshine or the rain. Yes, even in the rainy mist of the moment we should be thankful?"

"Yes, my sweet friend, I did."

"Connie, I was just about there. Pete was my security, and my mind didn't have to be on alert, especially since I'm not working."

"I know, Rosie, I thought maybe you could kick back and enjoy the estate and its amenities for a short time. But, tell me, who got shot? One of the neighbors, oil site worker?"

"No, no. It was a police officer from one of the local communities."

"A police officer. Oh, my. Is he alive?"

"Yes, he took a bullet to the upper thigh, and a Good Samaritan stopped and applied a tourniquet as the bullet had nicked an artery. He made it out of surgery, but still hospitalized."

"And the assailant? The shooter was already gone in that short period of time?"

"Yes, seems like it was instantaneous upon the officer stepping from his vehicle. It happened before he could release his door even to shut. It's all on his dash cam, and they have a good description of the pickup exiting the scene. And now my mind is more than active. It's on high-alert, and my fear level for Pete and Danny is off the chart!"

Connie, after a long released sigh, continues, "Rosie, I'm just sitting here in disbelief."

"Connie, can you think of anything in the house or at the estate that someone would be looking for? Something of value worth taking a chance like this over? Pete said the intruder had hidden in the stables until we left and then entered or searched the stables, and after he didn't locate anything, then entered the house. Either way, in my thinking, he was in the stables first because of the dirt. But no vehicle was seen on the security tapes."

"Rosie, you surely have your mind back in the detective mode."

As the girls chuckle, the conversation continues, but sitting only a few seats away, Connie and Rosie's conversation is getting significant notice and in an ominous way.

UNIDENTIFIED PASSENGER

"Yes, Sir, she's in my sight. I don't know. Looks like she's got a carry-on. I don't see a handbag. Maybe they're in her luggage. I'm trying, sir, believe me.

Hold on…

Okay, from the conversation I just heard, they seem to be aware of the intrusion into the Oklahoma residence. Yes, sir, I'm certain they're not at the estate, so she has them or possibly at the ranch. I can't imagine her leaving them unless she doesn't realize what she has. No, I haven't been there.

But, I'm so close to her now. I can have her carry-on in moments. It's up to you. Okay, Boss, it's your decision. Yes, sir, you're the boss!"

CONSTANCE LOUISE SINCLAIR

"Rosie, I have to go. I've got a call coming in. Love and hugs to you, also. See you later."

"Hello, Phillip, yes, you must have ESP. Yes, I'm headed home. When? At this very moment, I'm at LAX, now.

You have your corporate jet in Vegas enroute to Oklahoma? Oh, that would be wonderful, and they can be here that quickly?

That's ideal. As of the last time I checked the screen, I have a two hour wait.

No, Phillip, I have no objection to flying aboard a Citation Longitude. Textron Aviation was the only company from which Charles would consider purchasing, but the last jet of Textron's I have flown on was the Sovereign. I'm excited, and the flight will be very enjoyable and conjure many fond memories.

Yes, I'll head to flight support, now." She rises, smiles, and nods to the gentleman seated behind.

AMANDA BORDILLON

Amanda forcefully throws the dish cloth in the sink, leaves the dishes and heads to her room as she tries to grasp her feelings which are rapidly morphing to the surface in a quickened manner.

At the top of the stairs, she pauses as she glances toward Connie's room. She slowly realizes the depth of betrayal she feels from Connie has turned to scornful disdain as her heart aches for JJ. She diverts her steps to Connie's room and places her hand momentarily on the knob, pausing as if bracing herself before she enters. She leans in aggressively as if to challenge the darkness beyond, but the only thing she captures is her rising heart rate and tinges of emotion in her chest. Sitting on the bed, she places her arm across her face, falls back in hurtful exhaustion, and lets the heaviness in her limbs and muscles take control. Amanda doesn't fight sleep.

She awakes in brief confusion as her mind fights to recognize her surroundings. Amanda straightens and stands to exit the room when she notices the hydrangea embossed envelope bearing her name. Her senses are heightened almost to the point of being defensive as she has difficulty in advancing toward the desk.

Amanda hastily grasps the envelope and taps it on her hand. Ever so quickly, Connie's fragrance surrounds her. The all-too-familiar smell places Amanda in a weakened state, and feeling no further inner aggression, she pulls the contents of the envelope into the light as Connie's words flow from the page.

Amanda, I understand how unkind this must seem, but please listen. I realize at this moment you are feeling misled, deceived and even betrayed. But that is the furthest from my mind as I write. I hope and pray as time advances you will be able to possibly close your eyes and remember all the fun and lighthearted times we have shared. I don't know what an outsider would call us. Think about it, Amanda, please. I don't know, are we two members of a family that also share a friendship or two people, through a chance meeting, become friends because of a family?

You remember the Canvas and Cocktails party we attended, and you painted the Mustangs in the pasture and gave to me? And I painted the roses and hydrangea in my garden and gave to you? Well, if you check the wall above the desk, you will see I've taken the painting as I hold it dear in my heart...not only the Mustangs, but you, because your hands made the images.

Amanda, life is fragile and so unpredictable. You can't bend it like actors on a stage. No, for in life it's the moment of looking in a mirror and accepting your destiny or shattering the image and running before the shards of life can cut you to your very being.

My sweet child, I hope you can understand where I find myself.

All my love,

Connie

CONSTANCE LOUISE SINCLAIR

Connie, as she gratefully boards the Cessna jet, strangely feels Charles' unsettling presence as she turns and asks the pilot, "Am I to be the only passenger? Isn't that a little unusual?"

"Not really, ma'am. The previous guest's length of stay in Las Vegas permitted us to continue on to Los Angeles. I hope we meet your expectations on our flight to Oklahoma."

"I'm certain, you will. Thank you. Oh, how long will the flight take?"

"Upon take off, a little over two hours depending on wind speed."

"Thank you."

Connie leans back as she tries to shake the sensation of restlessness in both her body and mind. As fatigue gratefully wins, she watches the clouds and thinks, *do I let life take control and arrange its own details or is it better not to know?*

With a heavy sigh of resignation, her thoughts continue. *What is it with this need of control? Can I ever just let the symphony of life play on and play out? Playing and increasing to the crescendo, the crescendo of my life. Can I hold on as the drums beat, and the music makes its sweeping arc to the top and beyond or will the beyond always be out of my reach and continue to be what I'm chasing?*

It's the details of life, the mesmerizing idiosyncrasies of the notes in the song embedded for only a few to discern. These little places where only a maestro can take me, or maybe it's the notes I fail to hear that drive me crazy!

Why then do I have to hear every note? Is it better if some are not captured or does that mean it is open-ended, blank, incomplete?

Connie, Connie, Connie, can't you just let go of some of this control and what? Do all the why questions have to be tended and only to my satisfaction? All the blanks filled? What if there isn't an answer. Can I skip some of the points and just ellipsis my way through...???

I have, I have been trying. Trying to forget. Or...no, is it the opposite? I'm trying to recapture? It's maybe better to not know. Oh, Lord, I'm so lost, Father!

ROSIE REDMOND ROSEMAN

"Connie, you're home, and it's still daylight!"

"Yes, as I spoke with you, the other call I was receiving was Phillip Chapman. You remember Phillip? He was one of Charles' friends and also mine, and he and Joyce helped with the asset sale. Phillip was the one that brought the financial deficiency to my attention and stayed to the very end to help with everything, even the attorneys, and accountants."

"What was he calling about, business?"

Connie chuckles as she clearly tries to remember and confesses, "You know, that's funny, but I can't remember why he called. Anyway, he had a corporate jet in the area and offered me a speedy exit from my two or more hour wait, so I jumped at it."

"Well, la-tee-da, Miss Rich and Famous."

"Well, Miss Rosie Redmond Roseman, this Miss Rich and Famous is exhausted. The last few days have been harrowing. I have either been in the hauler on the road or frantically packing to catch a flight."

Rosie, walking towards the sink, adds, "I know, and then Pete and I dumped all the rest of this on you."

Connie's expression reverts to a look of anguish at Rosie's mention of Pete's question of valuables possibly enticing an intruder.

"Where are you going? Hey, wait. Connie, what's got that bee in your bonnet?"

"Come on, Rosie. My bedroom. You know I told you that I couldn't fathom anything of value to cause an intruder to enter?"

"Yes, so something comes to mind?"

"Well, Charles came to me again on the Cessna. As I sat and thought of him, I found myself rubbing my finger where my wedding set would be."

"So, you think the intruder broke in for your jewelry."

"Well, not exactly, because before the estate sale, I had given all my jewels, especially the ones from the safe to Phillip to have appraised. I was in such hope that they would bring enough to retain Magic and have him discharged from the asset portion of the sale. That was not the outcome as Phillip regretfully had to tell me that all my jewels were paste."

"Paste? But not your wedding set?"

"No, I couldn't or wouldn't part with my rings, and so I kept them from Phillip. Then, I went to work with you on the cleaning crew at the Petroleum Building, I knew they would only draw attention as they would most certainly be out of place on a scrubwoman. And also, I just kept looking at them after Phillip's disclosure that all were paste and feeling Charles' betrayal and wondering if they were part of the fraud that had been revealed. Then, one morning, as I dressed, I put my ring on and gave it a couple of crass turns and threw it in the drawer."

Rosie twirls her rings, waits anxiously with Connie in the master closet, and tries to peer over and around her, before impatience prompts her to protest, "Well, come on, are they there or gone?"

"No, they're here along with other items just as I left them. Nothing has been disturbed. What's going on? Maybe Pete's making too much out of this."

"Could be. This is his life, being a detective and observation is one of the biggest things that kinda gets to me," Rosie states weakly.

"What do you mean? Does he tell you that much about his work?"

"No, I'm talking personal observation. Personal observation of me!"

"Well, that should be flattering. Pete is your husband."

"Yes, but he notices when I have been to the hair stylist and get this, even when I have my nails done, or I get a new pair of shoes. What's up with that? I started to feel self-conscious, because there's no way I'm buying one pair of shoes if I'm buying. I've been hiding them under the bed and bringing out one pair at a time, so I can just tell him. No, not new as I've had them for weeks now."

"That's funny, Rosie. I'm so glad to be back home. I love you, girl!"

"Aw, I love you too, Connie."

CONSTANCE LOUISE SINCLAIR

Connie fills her cup as she admits, "I feel so much better after a night's sleep. I was so exhausted that I didn't even turn the radio on to help go to sleep."

"Yup and a second cup will help, also," Rosie agrees as she heads that way.

"I should call Geri and thank her for being so diligent in helping watch the estate before you and Pete came."

"Yes, good neighbors are hard to come by."

"I will drop her a thank you note in the mail. That will be more heartfelt, don't you think, Rosie?

"Did you get to meet her or you two speak on the phone?" Connie queries.

"Yes, I'm sure she would appreciate a note. I'd like to meet her, also, as I have never spoken with her."

"I might ask her for coffee after I have settled in a little. You never talked to Geri on the phone?"

"No, was I supposed to?"

"I just assumed you had as the last I spoke with her was the night I decided to go to California and visit Amanda. I've tried to call several times and then thought nothing more about it."

"Do you think that's odd?" Rosie snips.

"Yes and no. Out here, we think nothing about stopping at our neighbors if we see someone unexpected in the area or at their residence and asking what or who they are looking for. Why I am thinking it odd now, is the simple reason that they have livestock and can't intentionally leave without having someone there for them."

"I must confess," Rosie adds with a cringe on her face, "I have failed if I was supposed to have done that. If they show up on the security system coming and going from here, I take notice but otherwise, no."

"You aren't to blame. I should have continued to call until I received an answer. Being out of state is not an excuse. Anyway, you will like her, as you both share the same traits."

"Really, what?"

"Auburn hair and an incredible personality."

Rosie, with a resounding loud "Ha," asserts, "Henna number 8. As long as it comes in a bottle, I'll be Auburn."

"Come on, let's go up," chuckles Connie as she places her arm around her friend.

WILSON FARM

Connie drives as the ladies leave through the north entrance and turn west, Rosie is first to speak. "What a beautiful horse."

"Which one?"

"The polka dot one."

"Yes, she's a pinto. Wait until we turn back north at the section line, then look east when we get to the top of the hill, and you will see others. Some are paint, and others are pinto."

"I've never seen that many dotted horses before. They all look the same to me, except some have little dots and others big dots. What's the difference and how do they stay that clean in all this red dirt?"

Connie laughs, "I was raised with paints, the ones with the most distinct color pattern and they are my favorite, but the pintos with the smaller markings are quite striking. The Wilsons and their sons actively show through the American Paint Horse Association. My horse's name was Cherokee, and I could hang between his front legs when I was small, and he never offered to move. I had to learn all horses weren't that way."

As they turn up the drive, which seems to be steeper than the estate's drive, if that could be possible, Rosie grabs the cab of the truck's bar and straightens herself in the seat. The estate drive is blacktop, and this is red dirt which has washed in several areas from the recent rain. Connie is also maneuvering in her seat, but that seems to be most natural to her, as the front porch of the two story farm house comes into view.

Connie pulls past and turns toward the side of the house and parks outside the fenced area which looks like the place where most activity happens.

There's a small garage/barn to the front and side of the make-shift parking area and a bigger out building up the embankment to the east.

A big white dog announces their arrival.

Connie slides from the truck seat as the door opens, and an auburn haired petite lady with jeans and a plaid shirt exits and exclaims, "Connie, good to see ya'. Who's your friend?"

While Geri and Connie share a hug, Connie offers, "Geri, please meet Rosie."

Before Rosie can say her how-do-you-dos, Geri hugs her in the same greeting delivered to Connie, and Rosie thinks, *Holy moly. Either Connie has learned from Geri or Geri has learned from Connie.* As Rosie cajoles, "Yes, hugs all around. So nice to meet you."

They enter through the side door into the dining area with a long wooden table and high back chairs that seat ten.

"Come in. Let me take your jackets," Geri states as she places them on hooks beside the large entry door.

Rosie glances to her right and sees the kitchen as Geri pulls a chair from the table and offers, "Sit down, and I'll grab us some coffee. It has been far too long since we have visited."

Rosie is certain this is the main area of the home where business and pleasure are both shared, even though the living area is straight beyond the arched wall. Towards the kitchen, the wall has a big open faced stove with an attached flue. To the right of the kitchen entry is a rosewood phone with no dial but a handle on its side. Rosie is confident that the phone was used many years ago, but it still looks in perfect condition.

The table has placemats, and the items needed in day-to-day living are all present -- Salt, pepper, sugar, creamer, a holder of napkins, and a jelly compote filled with homemade jam. Rosie can't help but think that the crystal compote looks out of place from the other everyday items.

Geri returns with hot mugs of coffee and gets spoons from the buffet beside the table before she sits. Geri pulls the napkins toward their end of the table and bemoans, "Connie, I'm so sorry we were so irresponsible about watching your place for you."

"Geri, no apology necessary. I had tried to call, and then I just thought you and Rosie had probably spoken. Rosie and Pete agreed to stay at the estate. They came to my rescue and bailed me out of a situation where I had good intentions that went awry."

"Well, our intentions went awry, also, but not due to anything that we could have possibly ever thought of happening."

Connie with concern, chides, "Go on."

Geri scoots closer to the table and places both hands around her mug and confides while staring at the caramel colored liquid, "You remember Keri, Jake's girlfriend?"

"Yes," Connie answers while she looks at Rosie and advises, "Rosie, Jake is Geri and Ben's oldest."

Geri continues after a slight pause and a controlled breath. "Jake moved in with Keri several months back, and things had become rocky to the point of him leaving. Ben and I both didn't condone living like that without being married. Ben was very assertive when Jake showed up, and Jake turned back to his truck before even setting his things down and left in a huff. I tried to call, but he wouldn't pick up. He didn't show at work the next day or the next. Then we see on the news where Keri has been reported missing. I glanced towards Ben and saw him rubbing his forehead, but when he looked my way, he told me not to worry."

As Geri pauses and places her coffee to her mouth, she slowly rubs her right hand over the mug as if extracting every ounce of warmth to help the chills that are now more than obvious. Her bright eyes fade. "Jake came home unexpectedly and found Keri with another man. He had forced Keri to the truck, and that's why he fled after he fired the shot."

Connie, with grave concern, places her hand on Geri's shoulder and gently rubs in hopes of giving her friend a little empathy.

Geri, though shaken, straightens and continues. “Ben got up and went to the porch, and I followed. We both looked towards the lights of the city, and then Ben said, ‘I can remember sitting with my cousins and my Grandpa on this porch, and he would tell us to look to the lights and that one day, all this land would be houses and joined to the city, but Geri, that might not be such a good thing as it has become harder to protect yourself and your family.’ I nodded in agreement.

I came in and continued to call Jake. Ben comments, ‘Look Jake up on your phone app and if he has his phone on you should be able to locate him.’ I stare at the app as it spins, and it shows him just south of Piedmont on HW 4 toward Yukon. Ben assures, ‘when he stops, we can find him.’ I grabbed my jacket, and then a bulletin came on the TV revealing a Piedmont officer had been involved in a shooting, and the white male subject had left the scene in a red dually.”

Connie moans, “Oh, Geri.”

“I know,” counters Geri and then continues, “Ben and I raced to the truck and started to Yukon, still watching the GPS on my phone. Jake stopped at the park on Cornwell where he played Little League and was still there when we arrived.

Ben and I walked up to Jake’s truck, not knowing what we would find, but gratefully, he was okay, just sitting there with a forlorn look, and Ben said, ‘Son, come on let’s go.’

Oh, Connie that was the hardest thing we as parents had to do, was to walk our first born into the

Canadian County Sheriff's Office to let him turn himself in. But now, I thank God that we didn't get a call to go to the Medical Examiner's office to identify him. All things can be worked out just so long as he wasn't hurt."

Connie states as she touches her hand, "Yes, there are blessings in all things. Has he been charged, and if so, what are the charges?"

"They were quite lengthy at the beginning. Failure to stop, leaving the scene, resisting arrest, and failure to obey a lawful order, but the worst is shooting with intent to kill. Jake's preliminary hearing is the 25th."

"I'm so sorry," Connie states.

"Yes, but…"

"But what, Geri?"

"No one knows where Keri is!"

ROSIE REDMOND ROSEMAN

Rosie waits until Connie gives a last wave to Geri before Connie feels the look and inquires, "What is it? What are you thinking?"

"I'm thinking what a predicament that family is in. Did you get the feeling that there might be more to that story than she told?"

"No. Why so?" Connie quips.

"Where's Keri? Who is the other guy? Old boyfriend? Does she have family locally, and if so, are they in contact with them? This is more than a lover's spat, way more."

Connie eyes Rosie as she exclaims, "Boy, you're full of questions, aren't you?"

Rosie bristles a little and continues, "We have the creepy guy in your house just about the same time all this is going on, and you don't have questions?"

"I guess since you mention it, there could be a few questions I might like an answer to."

Connie goes silent.

Rosie glances her way several times and then asks the inevitable question. "What are you thinking?"

"I don't believe in happenstance. I think God places people in our paths for two reasons," informs Connie.

"Really!"

"Yes. Sometimes they are there as an answer to our need, even if we can't instantly see either the reason or the need at that season of our life."

"And number two?"

Connie continues, "Sometimes God places people in our paths, because we are to do something that will end up being an answer to their problem."

"And you automatically know this?"

"No, silly. God knows, and that's why we listen to that impulse, feeling, premonition, still voice or simply something that jumps into your mind for no reason. God gives us free will, but I know He directs our every step. It's just up to us to listen and react. It might be months before you will look back on that hard time of your life and see how one person was there to lead you through it.

Charles had an associate that I knew, but not in a close manner named Cyndy, and she sent cards and cards and cards that got me through some of the most gut-wrenching of days, and I know God touched her heart and thus saved me, literally, from drowning in grief. Thank you, Lord, for Cyndy!"

JEREMIAH JASON PAIGE

"Doug, are you here?"

"Yes, what's up?"

JJ, holding his hand out, grumbles, "Look what I picked up. Why are the guys throwing their gum wrappers on the ground?"

CONSTANCE LOUISE SINCLAIR

The drive is short, but not as familiar as it possibly should have been. Sleep has evaded Connie, and the feeling for a need, a purpose, is revisiting her nightly.

The silence of the early morning lays as thick as the dew on the stately tombstones. The clang of the entry gate at the Zion cemetery unsettles birds waking to their day, and they lift hastily in flight.

Walking forward, Connie reads the names of her family with each name bringing her a smile. Aunt Geraldine, Aunt Mae, Uncle Carl, Uncle Bill, Grandma and Grandpa, Aunt Blanche. Yes, each being memorialized by their sedentary pillars.

Her pace slows as she almost halts before forcefully stepping across the narrow path as Connie brings her gaze to the black stone that reads:

CHARLES DAVID SINCLAIR
February 4, 2014

The crunch of the dry, brittle grass does nothing to elevate her spirit as she lets her mind remember the days after Charles' death. She remembers all the months it took to get her where she could visit and not feel the need to lay prostrate on the ground. Yes, lay and let her body melt into the grave below, melt into the grave with Charles.

Charles, I'm here. I know it has been so long, I know, but I heard you last night when you spoke my name. You startled me awake and took my breath away. I miss you so much.

Charles, when you get married as young as we did, you would expect to make it to our golden anniversary, wouldn't you? You would believe that our forever would still be in the years to come. But the years to come are memories we haven't lived, and I'm the only one living them and only in my mind.

You know, sweetheart, the painful thing is when I allow the memories to advance past the present. I try to capture them, capture the memories, the memories of our lives in the future...the future that should have been. Oh, Charles, that's when I relapse to the beginning and start the journey once more.

I'm here, because I know you are trying to tell me something. I'm frightened. What is it Charles, what is it?

OFFICE OF DETECTIVE DANIEL DOBBINS OKLAHOMA CITY POLICE DEPARTMENT

Pete enters Detective Dobbins office to find him on the phone. Danny motions to Pete to sit down, but Pete prefers to pace as he jiggles the change in his pocket.

Danny hurriedly states, "I'll have to call you back," as he places the phone in its cradle.

"What's going on, Pete?"

"I wish I knew, Danny. You know, Rosie and I are at the Sinclair estate while Connie was in California."

"Yes, and that's a problem?"

"No, but Connie has returned, and I don't think it's safe to leave her alone. I don't feel comfortable moving back to our apartment here in the city."

"What's happened, Pete? Something has to make you feel that way."

"I just need to bounce some things off of you and see if you come to the same conclusion before I upset everyone."

"Upset who?"

"Connie and Rosie."

"Why, again, are you there? You were just house sitting for Mrs. Sinclair, weren't you?"

"Yes, we were supposed to make the estate available to the technicians monitoring the prototype installed on the Sinclair well sites, but then the earthquakes happened, and questions about the new equipment started to surface. People became jumpy thinking the prototype was part of the injection well system the state has curtailed."

"Was it all verbal, or was there a definite situation?"

"No, just questions and some pointed accusations that the Sinclair estate was not following the same mandates as other well owners," Pete states as he still paces.

"But you addressed their concerns, didn't you?"

"No. Not personally. Rosie was the one at the end of the interrogation by the neighbors, and she was at a loss as she doesn't know enough about oil sites and this particular situation to do much good. That's when I asked her to close the front gates when I was away and utilize the intercom system. It was just a precaution at the time, or so I thought, until a few days later."

Danny leans forward in his chair and asks, "What happened then?"

Pete runs his hand through his hair once again as he sits in one of the adjoining chairs and continues, "That's when I discovered someone had been in the house by way of the back entry. He rifled through a desk drawer, and some papers were disturbed. I could find nothing else, but he entered several of the rooms in the house, and the surveillance cameras never caught his face."

"Caucasian?"

"Yes, as far as I could tell the pictures were not clear, but he was definitely up to no good."

"How so?"

"Avoided eye contact with cameras, zippered jacket with hoodie pulled up and was gloved. And Danny…"

"What?"

"There was a bulge under his jacket, so I think he was armed."

"Which side?"

"Neither, the back."

"So we can't tell by that which hand is dominant. What about hair color?"

"No, couldn't see."

"Has Rosie noticed any strange vehicles in the area?"

"Not that easy, Danny. We haven't been out there that long. The estate is only a short distance from Northwest Highway, and there is a large concentration of oil related vehicles coming and going. Believe me, I have gone through every scenario I can think of and keep coming up with nothing."

Danny continues, "Let's get the Canadian County Sheriff's Office in on this, or have you already?"

"Not officially. I introduced and identified myself as an Oklahoma City Police Department Detective to a deputy that lives in the area. I asked if he was aware of any reports of suspicious persons, but I didn't go any further regarding the exact reason for my inquiry."

Danny, as he rises from his chair and walks around his desk, counters, “This wasn’t a snatch and grab, because I’ve been in that house at your wedding and there are several items would be accessible immediately upon his entry into the residence. No, he was looking for something specific. You have any idea what it was?”

“No. I had Rosie ask Connie when she spoke with her before she headed back to Oklahoma and Connie could think of nothing except her wedding set.”

“And?”

“It was still there when she checked,” states Pete.

Danny turns toward Pete and questions, “If he was going through the desk, it could be something financial or business related. Where does Mrs. Sinclair keep all that?”

Pete stands and states as he takes a deep breath, “I have no idea, but don’t rich people have attorneys and accountants that handle all that?”

ROSIE REDMOND ROSEMAN

"Connie, where are you?

Good, you're on your way home. I was worried. You were gone when I came down this morning, and you didn't leave a note on the pad.

Okay, Pete called, and he wants to talk to us both. He's on his way to the estate now."

PETER ROSEMAN

"Is Connie here?"

"Pete, what is it? You are so…so in work mode."

"I know, sweetheart. I can't turn it off, at least when there is a reason. Where is Connie? Were you able to contact her?"

"Yes, she couldn't sleep, so she went to see Charles."

"Oh."

"I bet that's her now," states Rosie as they hear the back door.

"What's going on, Pete?" Connie chides as she enters a little winded and gets coffee. I went to see Charles, in hopes some of this would become clear.

She offers Pete and Rosie mugs. Each accepts, and the ladies sit at the bar while Pete stands at the end.

"Rosie, I know you are packing us up to go back to our apartment, but I think we need to stay a little longer," Pete states in an assertive voice.

Rosie immediately defends her packing and asserts, "We were asked to help Connie, and now she's home, so we need to give her her space and leave."

Pete advances as he touches Rosie and answers in a softened tone, "I know, but there is more to our intruder than I have told you."

Rosie gasps as she looks toward Connie, but Connie is lost in the unsettling presence of Charles.

AMANDA BORDILLON

It is wet, dark, and cold, the effects of the last rain. A fine mist hangs which gives an ominous sensation. Doug and JJ are at a meeting concerning the wild Mustangs, and Amanda declined their invitation to go. She makes her way to the stable to check on Magic before she grabs a book and calls it an early night. Amanda enters, and as she turns, she is met with resistance.

"Eyes ahead," is all she hears as she feels the pressure to her back prodding her forward. Amanda glances over her shoulder and sees Magic secure in his stall and then with hope, looks toward the bunkhouse praying Miguel or one of the other ranch hands would suddenly appear. Slowing, she feels the prod pressing her forward.

DOUGLAS HARTLY

"Still no answer. Why isn't she picking up? JJ, I think we better head home."

JEREMIAH JASON PAIGE

The gravel forcefully flies as JJ applies the brakes, and both men jump from the truck at the back of the house. Amanda has never answered her phone after repeated calls during their hasty drive to the ranch, and both men are beyond rational thoughts.

Doug is first to the sunroom door which fails to yield. JJ immediately heads to the front as he hollers for Doug to get the keys from the truck.

After swift entry, both men call out to Amanda. Doug maneuvers the steps multiple at a time, and JJ continues the search of the downstairs. He sees nothing in the living area and kitchen, as he checks the sunroom door and sees the deadbolt engaged. Returning, he halts in the kitchen as he hears movement behind the bar. He advances quickly and sees Amanda subdued on the floor, hands and feet bound, mouth taped. He slides across the wooden floor to her side as he shouts, "Doug, in here!"

Doug is by their side in a flash, helps JJ lift Amanda and quickly moves her into his embrace.

JJ slashes the binding on her ankles as Doug resists releasing her to let JJ undo her wrists but then quickly yields as he removes the last hindrance from her mouth.

Amanda goes limp as Doug carries her to the sunroom and places her on the settee.

JJ brings a cloth, and Doug softly and slowly washes her forehead, cheeks, and mouth. Amanda cries.

JEREMIAH JASON PAIGE

"The Sheriff's Office has someone on their way," states JJ as he continually walks the length of the room.

"Doug, how could this have happened? What could we have that someone would go to this length to obtain?

Where is Miguel and the others? I want to talk to them, and right now! Do you think they are doing something illegal that could have brought this about?

I should have confronted Miguel when I found that trash by the stables. It has to be someone they let on the ranch without us knowing. I'm thinking that drone we found might not have been a kid's toy, but a spy tool!"

LOS ANGELES COUNTY SHERIFF'S DEPUTY

"I understand JJ, believe me," states Dwayne. "And I'm glad I was on duty when the call came in. We'll get to the bottom of this. Give us a little more time outside, and then we'll check back with you before we leave in case you think of anything else."

JJ gratefully shakes Dwayne's hand as he looks to Amanda still in the arms of Doug. "Will it be okay if Amanda goes on up to bed? Is there any more you need from her?"

"No, I'm good." Looking to Amanda, Dwayne consoles, "You get some rest, and I want you to know you were very brave when you fought back. Some people think courage is the absence of fear, but I know from experience that once you face fear, courage is all you have left."

AMANDA BORDILLON

Standing at the base of the stairs, still huddled in the afghan, Amanda lifts her foot to the first step, and then stops and begs, "I can't. I can't go up there. I can't sleep upstairs alone. After Mother left, I got used to it but I've had Connie with me these last months just a few rooms away, but now, I can't, just can't."

LOS ANGELES COUNTY SHERIFF'S DEPUTY

Dwayne enters and speaks to JJ and informs, "JJ, we're leaving, but we'll be back tomorrow for follow up and check the area in the daylight. Jerry located this," Dwayne lifts a plastic bag as Doug and JJ inch closer.

Doug gulps, "A cell phone? Where did you find that?"

"Up by the stables where Amanda tried to take her stand. Does it look familiar? It isn't one of yours?" asks Dwayne.

Doug looking toward JJ, continues, "No, but did you talk to Miguel and the others. Is it theirs?"

"Yes, we spoke with them, and right now I'm inclined to believe they are not a part of this."

JJ queries, "What about the phone? They knew nothing on the phone?"

"No, they stated they haven't seen it before. I'll take it to our lab people and get their determination. It looks like the last text was received earlier this evening."

Doug questions, "And what was it? Can you tell us?"

"Yes, because I'm hoping you might be able to help me with it."

JJ moves closer to Dwayne and Doug as Dwayne informs, "Leave remember DAK."

JJ slowly repeats, "DAK? Is that initials?

Dwayne shakes his head and admits, "I'm not certain. That doesn't mean anything to you?"

"No, I wish it did. DAK?"

CONSTANCE LOUISE SINCLAIR

Connie parks at Penn Square Mall, and as she exits her car, she finds herself checking her surroundings.

She tries to rationalize the swiftly occurring events and Pete's admission of resistance to leaving her alone at the estate.

Could this all be true? Why are Rosie and Pete both rushing to the conclusion that this is all towards me? Is it not so unlikely to think that this might have something to do with Pete's job and their stay at the estate? That has to be it.

ROSIE REDMOND ROSEMAN

"Pete, so where's the footage of the guy entering the house? Is it here? I'd like to see it."

"You can't see much. He was hooded and had gloves on and never looked directly into the camera. Every indication is that he has done this before and knows how to evade being seen."

Rosie, in a persistent, undaunted voice, taunts, "Yes, but you know it's always better to have more eyes in case one person sees something the other misses."

"Well, I've done this a few years, so I tend not to 'miss' much," states Pete with an emphasis on "miss" as he sees the look in Rosie's eyes. "But you're not going to give up, are you?"

Rosie continues her gaze toward him until she sees the softening of his face and Pete gasps, "Come on."

Rosie, happily seated, watches while Pete leans against the opposite side of the desk with satisfaction that nothing more could be learned by viewing it again with her.

Rosie grabs a pad and scribbles, "left handed."

Pete leans back a little to see what she has written, but Rosie strategically rests her arm on the pad. Pete wrinkles his brow as he tries to determine if this was intentional on Rosie's part. "Surely not??"

Again she scribbles, "Shoelaces."

At this, Pete turns toward the screen, wondering what he could have overlooked. Maybe one thing, but now two items. Without a doubt, she is noticing the same things he did, but he just doesn't feel the need to jot things down.

A third time she jots, and Pete is comfortably situated right there to see Rosie write, "Expensive shoes."

Pete states in an escalated voice, "Expensive shoes!"

Rosie is quick to answer, "Yes, Sir. And believe me, I know shoes!"

Returning to the recording, Rosie, once again, moves her pencil to the pad and writes, "Right leg slight drag, doesn't lift completely."

Rosie leans back from the computer, and Pete takes the opportunity to snatch the pad from the desk and reads aloud, "Left handed. There is no way you can tell that."

Rosie with an exhaled breath and one nod of the head states, "Going up the stairs, he led with his left foot, and when he flipped the switch, he used his left hand."

"I don't think that can be used as a determining factor," chides Pete crisply.

"Oh really, we'll see on our way down which leg you lead with," offers Rosie.

Pete continues down the list, "Shoelaces? What's up with that?"

"Just that the laces aren't tied and tucked in the top of the shoes."

Pete counters, "I think that's a little stretch as evidence."

Rosie announces, "You might be right, and I don't know how rare this is, but if all four of these are present in one person, it will lead me to look a little closer at him as a suspect."

Pete continues, "Well, I'll give you this next one only after I watch the film once more. But if he does favor his right foot, then all of these together are definitely pertinent."

Even before Pete hits the play button to review the security footage, he is wishing he isn't going to have to make that confessional call to Danny.

PETER ROSEMAN

"Danny, it's me. Yeah, I wanted to tell you that there are a few little peculiar irregularities about our intruder that have surfaced.

ROSIE REDMOND ROSEMAN

"Connie, you're back. Can we talk?"

"Sure, what's up?"

"I wanted to talk with you about Jake."

Connie stops and turns with her face askew.

Rosie continues, "You know, the son of Geri and Ben, your neighbors?"

"I'm aware of who Jake is. Are you still thinking there is more to learn about what has happened? The shooting of that police officer?"

"Well, kinda, but more precisely about his appearance."

Connie walks toward the bar and places her jacket over the chair. "What do you want to know? You've seen him in that television clip at his arraignment. Sandy hair about six foot."

Rosie joins Connie and asks, "What about his shoes?"

Connie stares at the glassware in the breakfront as she thinks, "You mean his boots? I don't believe I've ever seen him in anything but boots."

"Okay, do you know if he is left handed?"

"I have no idea. What are you getting at?

"Well, just thinking a little," continues Rosie, "and…"

Connie cutting in, boldly states, "You remind me of the mode you were in at the Petroleum Tower when you found Cassie Walters dead. You know, all the stuff you get to rolling around in your head."

Rosie seats herself next to Connie as she continues, “I suppose I am. I guess I’m back to all the wondering I do when things aren’t as they should be.”

CONSTANCE LOUISE SINCLAIR

"Rosie, I'm going to check the mail. You haven't got it yet, have you?"

"No, but I will if you want."

"I'm good," replies Connie, "I shouldn't have even asked. It's not like an extra trip to the mailbox would do me any harm.

Hey, I'll be in the garden, also. Check and see if any flowers are making an appearance," hollers Connie.

"If Danny insists we remain here much longer, I'm tempted to have our mail delivered back out here. I shouldn't have had the forward stopped when he said we were going back to the apartment. We'll see," replies Rosie with a heavy sigh.

Rosie hears the door and thinks that's odd. "Connie! Connie, is that you?" as she walks to the front of the house.

Rosie sees Connie with a concerned look on her face and blurts, "Why are you back so quickly?"

Rosie stops by Connie's side at the entryway table as Connie is holding a small manila package. "What is it?"

Connie slowly states, "I don't know, but it's addressed to Charles and return address is Member Service Center, Nashville, Tennessee."

Rosie urges Connie, "Open it. It looks thick."

"Rosie, you open it. My heart is pounding."

"Okay, okay. Give it here."

Connie continues, "Do you know how eerie it feels to see something addressed to Charles?"

"No, I don't."

"Oh, Rosie. I just went to the cemetery and asked Charles what he was trying to tell me with these uneasy feelings he's sending. It just keeps me anxious after every episode."

Rosie partially tears the end of the envelope and then turns before continuing, "Are you thinking Charles is answering your question?"

"Well, we will soon see after you open that," cautions Connie.

Connie draws closer as Rosie is still holding the package and adds, "Why did you stop?"

Rosie stammers, "Look at the postmark. It's stamped November 20, 2014."

Connie counters, "It can't be. Three years ago?"

Connie takes the package from Rosie, checks the date, finishes opening before letting the contents hit the entryway table.

Both stand as they stare at a key ring containing keys. Connie lifts them as she fingers through and sees Charles' initial coin.

"Rosie, these are Charles'."

"Are you sure? How do you know for certain?"

"This is Charles' coin. See, it has his initial on it. He always carried one in his pocket with his change. I originally was under the impression that he used it when he played golf as a place marker. But now…"

Rosie quickly jumps in, "But now what? What makes you doubt that isn't still true?"

Connie places her hand to her face as she tries to clarify all this and confides, "When I was first trying to be in Amanda's life, Doug called and said Amanda was despondent and had stopped attending Magic's trials. He said he was past worry about her and had moved to overly concerned. He asked if I could return to California to help ground her, so I went."

"Okay, Amanda had one?"

"Well, yes and no. Upon arriving at the ranch, I was a little hesitant of Amanda's reception to my unannounced visit, so I left everything in the car. Luggage, purse and even keys in the ignition. By the end of the day, she invited me to stay instead of going to a hotel. Upon bringing in everything, I tossed my bag on the end of the couch, and it fell to the floor. Amanda picked up my purse and placed it on the ottoman along with lip gloss, mints, and a few coins."

"So, this was in with those coins?"

"No," states Connie.

Rosie, more than a little frustrated, turns in a circle and exclaims, "Holy moly!"

"Okay," states Connie. "I'm getting there."

"A few days later, I had come down and was getting coffee. Amanda was in the sunroom and lying beside the coffee were some coins and among them was this coin. I thought it strange, and as I went to pull them into my palm, Amanda stopped me."

"Stopped you! Physically stopped you?"

"Well, yes. Amanda placed her hand on my forearm, and as I turned, she placed an identical coin beside the one on the counter as the tears flowed.

It seems Amanda had found the extra coins under the ottoman, and they had, evidently, fallen from my purse that first night and lay undetected until she came across them.

Amanda said she placed them beside the coffee for me and then after a moment's thought, ran to her mother's room where she remembered seeing a similar coin in her mother's jewelry.

She had not realized it was Charles', until she saw the one from my purse."

"So, that makes two coins, and this is a third. But the keys, were they lost and then mailed in return? That doesn't explain the date, though," counters Rosie.

"No, but the address isn't our home address."

Rosie snatches the envelope and questions, "Whose address is this?"

"It's close to Charles office address, but numerals are not correct."

"You're thinking it has been at the post office all this time?"

"I don't know how that works, but my guess is it has been," states Connie.

Rosie, still feeling confused, complains, "Charles mails himself his own keys and gets the wrong address? Not likely in my estimation."

Connie shakes her head as if to agree to the unlikelihood.

Rosie states, "So you agree?"

"Yes," assures Connie. "It can't be Rosie. Charles couldn't have sent these."

"How can you be so sure?" replies Rosie.

Connie in a lowered voice as she turns toward the window, moans, "Because Charles died in February!"

UNIDENTIFIED ASSAILANT

"I understand. I was just going by what you told me."

"What?"

"Okay, Boss, I saw that."

DOUGLAS HARTLY

"If we haven't heard something from the Sheriff's Office by this afternoon, I'm calling them before it gets too late," exclaims JJ.

Looking at JJ, Doug asks, "Have you thought of anyone with those initials that you or the ranch has an association with?"

"No, but I haven't spoken to Amanda," replies JJ.

Doug clinches his jaw and bristles.

JJ notices and adds, "What is it, Doug?"

"Amanda has been through enough without having her relive last evening."

"I know, Doug, I know."

Doug counters briskly, as he stands eye to eye with JJ and asserts, "She heard the same thing we did. She was right here when Dwayne told us what the last message said, so leave her alone!"

"But she may have thought of someone since then," JJ exclaims.

JJ turns and walks away hoping to regain his composure and slow his breathing as he can't believe Doug is confronting him in this manner.

Keeping a distance and not looking at Doug, JJ strives to regain mental calmness as he slowly answers, "Okay Doug, I understand where you are coming from. You don't need to prove anything to me. I know you want nothing more than to protect Amanda, and I'm right there with you. It can wait until we have heard from Dwayne."

CONSTANCE LOUISE SINCLAIR

"Rosie, how long have we been standing here? Well, at least, how long have I been standing and you pacing?"

"I don't know. I just don't know what is so important that you have and someone wants!"

Connie with a sigh repeats, "I still think it could have something to do with Pete, because his job would be conducive to this sort of thing."

Rosie stops and joins Connie at the kitchen bar and instructs, "Close your eyes."

Connie, a little flustered, challenges, "Why. What are you going to do?"

Rosie pulls a barstool away from the counter and instructs, "Sit down."

Connie backs two paces and in an apprehensive voice exclaims, "No way. Not until you tell me what you are going to do!"

"Nothing. I'm not going to touch you. I just want you to think clearly, and the best way to do that is too close your mind to outside distractions so close your eyes as I go over what we do and don't know."

Connie willingly, but cautiously advances as she questions, "Would it have hurt you to tell me that first?"

"Geez," asserts Rosie. "Are you ready?"

Connie, eyes closed and hands laying on the bar with intertwined fingers, answers in a solemn voice, "Yes, I am, officer!"

"Okay. You speak with Doug, and you leave for California. Anything suspicious going on during that time?"

"No."

"You ask the Wilsons to watch your place. You call and ask Pete and me to house sit. We have earthquakes, and your neighbors become concerned over the prototype. Am I missing anything? Hello, feel free to jump in here anytime!" Rosie complains.

Connie opens her eyes and answers, "I tried to call Ben and Geri but never got ahold of them. Did Geri explain that away?"

"No, she didn't. Where's that pad that is supposed to be on the bar?"

Connie points, and Rosie grabs it off the desk.

"Okay, I'm writing that down. This is too much to keep in my head."

Rosie comes back to the bar with pen and paper and jots the memo down.

Rosie, as she glances at Connie, continues, "Close your eyes!"

Connie counters with, "This feels like an interrogation instead of a fact finding process."

Ignoring Connie, Rosie coaxes, "You call, and I tell you about the earthquakes, and you get home, and we visit the Wilsons and hear about Jake and Keri." Rosie writes, "More to that story!"

Connie opens her eyes and adds, "You forgot about the guy searching the house."

"No, I didn't. He's the whole reason we are doing this. What could he be looking for? We know he entered your bedroom, and we determined he had left your wedding rings, but what else of value is there?"

Connie suddenly inhales an, "Aww" sound.

Rosie jumps forward and exclaims, "What. You just thought of something. What else is up there?"

Connie leaps from her stool and answers, "Magic's papers!"

Rosie is in fast pursuit and enters Connie's bedroom as she sees Connie enter her closet. Rosie scoffs, "You keep his papers in your closet?"

"Not exactly. They were in my suitcase, and when I unpacked, I pushed the envelope in beside my jewelry chest. They fit so snugly, I guess I forgot them until now. But see, they are still here. Oh Rosie, do you think this has to do with Magic?"

"You have half ownership, and Doug has the other half. Can you think of any reason someone would try and steal Magic's ownership documents? We ruled out the jewelry."

"Yes," Connie answers as she is the one now pacing.

Rosie continues the barrage of questions. "Anything connected to the keys?"

"I don't think so. Oh, I don't know!"

"Okay honey, settle down. Was there any time you were with Charles when he used the keys in any manner?"

"No. Never," states Connie in a defeated tone.

"And the only other time anyone has been in here was Ludlow to steal the files off Charles' computer."

Rosie continues, "So, what about anything to do with the prototype? Anything you can associate with that?"

No answer is forthcoming from Connie as Rosie seems undeterred and continues aggressivly, "Can you think of any connection to Magic and racing? Did Charles keep records on Magic and finances?"

Connie backs and shakes her head. "I might call Doug, but not JJ," as their final conversation is relived in her mind.

"Connie, Connie! Did you hear me?"

Connie in a slow drawn out tone answers, "I never told you about our last meeting, did I?"

Connie lowers her voice and walks to the doors exiting to the balcony as she continues the journey into her last day at the Bordillon ranch.

PETER ROSEMAN

"No wonder Connie is resting. It sounds like she is completely overwhelmed, not only by Charles, but this whole turn of events. Did she call?"

Rosie shakes her head as she lets out a long breath and admits, "No. It seems, as she was leaving, JJ continued to plead with her, she said, her pace momentarily ceased as he touched her arm. She advanced a few steps only to halt as he spoke her name. She weakened a moment, and then she turned his direction to only hold her hand, palm up in a way that seemed to convey the conversation was over."

"How can two people do that to each other?" Pete accuses.

"I don't know. That's when Connie fell to pieces."

CONSTANCE LOUISE SINCLAIR

"Hey, Pete, you're home. Have a good day? Oh, is that something you don't ask a law enforcement officer?"

Rosie walks to Connie, hugs her and asks, "Have you decided anything?"

"No, not exactly. But, I keep telling myself I can do this."

Pete intervenes and exclaims, "Are you certain?"

"Yes, Pete. I talk the talk, I just need to walk the walk and take control of my life, so that should cover all aspects, not just the ones I choose to deal with."

"Whatever you feel like doing is fine," states Rosie.

Connie moves to the desk, picks up her phone and returns to the bar.

"Hello, Doug?"

"Yes, Connie. So happy to hear from you. All well with you?" Doug inquires as he heads to catch JJ before he drives off.

"Yes and no."

"Really. Could you hold on a minute until I change locations?"

Doug frantically waves JJ from his pickup as he mouths, "Connie"

JJ jumps from the truck as it continues its roll to a stop, and both men converge at the portico.

"Okay, Connie, I just wanted to get inside the stable so I could hear you better."

JJ leans in as Doug holds the phone away from his ear.

"You said you are doing well?"

"Not exactly. That's why I called. Rosie and Pete are still at the estate for the time being and…you know what, Doug, would you mind if I put you on speaker?"

"Okay, hello, Rosie and Pete. Now, what's all this about?"

"There has been a strange occurrence of events that leads me to ask if you know of any reason why Magic's ownership would be something someone would wish to obtain?"

"No, Connie. I haven't had anyone contact me concerning purchasing stakes in Magic. Who contacted you?"

"No one, Doug. That's why we are calling because, because, oh Pete will you continue?"

"Doug, we had an uninvited guest a few weeks back and…"

"Wow, Pete, hold on, I'm putting you on speaker also, as I want JJ to hear this."

JJ answers, "I'm here. Go ahead Pete. Who was it?"

Rosie turns her complete attention to Connie as soon as she hears JJ's voice. She tries to read Connie, but is unable as Connie seems adverse to any emotion.

"As I stated, he was uninvited, and he entered through the back entrance which was unlocked, but still burglary none the less."

"What did he take?"

"It happened about a week before Connie came home, and it was one of the determining factors that brought her back."

JJ interjects, "I was unaware of that determining factor."

Pete briskly answers, "Rosie didn't know, thus Connie didn't know until I was told Connie had started this direction the night before she left. Rosie hadn't had the opportunity to speak with Connie again until she was at the airport waiting to board."

Doug, trying to intervene, interjects, "Was anyone home?"

"No, thank goodness. I had come home early, and noticed someone had entered. I checked the house but found nothing until I checked the security camera."

"So has he been identified? What did he take?"

"Nothing that we can determine. We just know that he is left handed and possibly favors his right foot."

Rosie jumps in at that and announces, "Not possibly. He favors his right foot."

Doug states, "Pete, we had an episode at the ranch almost like that. Amanda was alone, and someone jumped her while she was in the stables checking on Magic."

Connie at hearing this asks, "She wasn't hurt? He didn't hurt her? The monster. What does he want? Oh, Pete, you were right. It's me, it's me. I just want this over, please let it be over."

Rosie shows her concern for Connie as she had only a few hours earlier. Rosie knows Connie wants to show her strength and control over her life, but how much can one person battle alone, all alone as the shadows hover?

Doug looks to JJ whose head is lowered in response to Connie's arduous outcry.

Rosie leads Connie toward the back as they share a tearful embrace and Rosie thinks, *"Connie, oh Connie, can't you realize what Pete and I know to be true, that you and JJ are meant to be with each other. I know you keep revisiting the deep pain you suffer from the loss of Charles, but after being told of Amanda's encounter, will your self-determined bravery be enough to sustain you? Can't you see what JJ has to offer? JJ can bolster your strength and give you his steady heart which, not only holds his undying love, but is still waiting. Can't you just recognize it and embrace it?"*

Rosie glances back to Pete as he adds, "It easily could have been the same perp that entered here. Sounds like you've got a little more to go on than we do, but not much."

Pete continues, "I think this is the break we need. Give me his description?"

"No description, Amanda didn't get a look at him. It was dark, and he took her by surprise."

"Nothing? Right or left handed?

"No, but she did hear his voice but only a few words. Amanda thinks he had a gun as she felt pressure on her back. She fought him briefly outside the stables before he got her subdued and in the house.

The Sheriff's Office found his phone at the location where Amanda tried to flee."

"Great news. So they are checking that lead?"

"It was a burner, and there was a text message from another burner phone."

"What did the text say?"

"Immediately that night, Dwayne, one of the deputies told us it just said, 'Leave remember DAK.' And wanted to know if that meant anything to us."

Pete looks to Connie and asks, "DAK, Connie, do you know anyone with the initials DAK?"

"Wait, Pete, there's more."

"What?"

"Their tech people said it was initials but not of a person, it's an acronym like a slang used in tweets and text messages. So the whole message was actually, 'Leave-remember, deny any knowledge'."

"Deny any knowledge! That tells me one thing."

"What's that, Pete?"

"Whoever is the head of this is way up the food chain and doesn't care to be involved in any manner. That still doesn't make much sense, though."

"It didn't to us, either, but then the lab was able to get the first message retrieved, and it said, 'Boss, someone's home!'"

Connie grabs Pete's arm and gasps, "Oh, no! Oh, my! I have chills. It's Charles, and he's verifying my thought. I was so close."

JJ in his protecting voice, not only wanting to exact revenge for Amanda, but also wanting to rush to Connie, questions, "Who is it, Connie? Tell me, who is it?

"JJ, I don't know, but he was behind me at the terminal as I spoke with Phillip. I heard him say, 'But Boss, I'm so close. Okay, Boss.' As I rose to head to Flight Services, I glanced his way and nodded."

Pete asks, "What did he look like?"

"Strange eyes, narrow, cold, somehow unyielding. He gave no acknowledgment to my departure."

DETECTIVE DANIEL DOBBINS

"Pete, there you are. I've been looking for you. Why were you late this morning? You didn't answer your cell, so I checked to see if you caught a call during the night."

"Sorry, Danny, I was in forensics, talking with Al about the keys."

"What did you find out?"

"It seems this Members Services Center is a drop for lost keys. The key chain held information with the Center's P.O. Box on it. If your keys are lost, they check the corresponding number and get your keys back to you."

"That's interesting. Hum."

"Hum, what, Danny?"

"When I was in corrections before making the department, we used chits but in a different manner. We had chits with our keys, and they were used to keep up with evidence and such."

"You're right. We had chits with our badge numbers on them, and we had to leave a chit for keys, files, etc. That way we didn't break the chain of evidence if the case when to court."

"Danny, where you off to?"

JEREMIAH JASON PAIGE

"Doug, Dwayne is on his way here with the Undersheriff and has some information.

Let's hope this is coming to a quick end and some reassurance, along with a little peace, might be returned to us."

Doug turns and kicks at the straw on the floor and groans, "I'm certainly not enthusiastic about telling one law enforcement agency what we learned days ago from another law enforcement officer, are you? If so, be my guest, as I don't even know where to begin."

JJ nods in agreement and admits, "Now that you put it that way, let's just see what they have to tell us."

DEPUTY SHERIFF DWAYNE JOHNSON

"JJ, Amanda told us you were out here. This is Undersheriff Lynn Morris. Lynn, this is JJ Paige and Douglas Hartly."

"Please, call me Doug."

"Nice to meet you, gentlemen. I wanted to come out with Dwayne and let you folks know that the Los Angeles County Sheriff's Office is taking this event seriously. This home invasion could have been a lot worse, but thankfully it wasn't."

"Our sentiments exactly," agrees Doug.

"We have increased patrol coverage to help Dwayne break this area into more controllable zones, and I hope this gives you some bit of comfort."

JJ states, "Yes, we appreciate that very much."

"JJ said you had further questions for us?"

"Yes, I do, but before I ask them, there is some information I need to relate to you.

I know you are aware of the text messages and the phones being burners."

"Yes, and Dwayne told us that unless the other phone was turned back on you had no hope of tracing it back to anyone."

"That is partially correct."

Doug and JJ glance at each other as JJ asks, "So you know who the phone belongs to?"

"No, but the serial number on the phone gives us an additional avenue. The exact location where the phone was purchased can be determined."

JJ adds, most enthusiastically, "And if that is determined then security footage could have caught the transaction. So you know who purchased it?"

Undersheriff Morris states, "Yes and no. We have determined the point of sale and are asking assistance from the jurisdictional law enforcement agency to try and obtain that information."

Doug questions, "It wasn't purchased in LA County?"

"No, it wasn't even purchased in our state, much less our county."

Doug takes a step back as his perplexed look shows on his face. JJ, though, seems conflicted as he presses his lips together in a slight grimace.

The Undersheriff continues, "The phone was purchased in Oklahoma."

Doug exclaims, "Oklahoma!" JJ offers no opinion and turns away from the conversation.

"That brings me to my next question. Mr. Paige, could I have your attention, once more?"

"Who is the owner of the horse trailer parked next to the stables?

Both JJ and Doug have an uneasy feeling as if they are being led down a slippery slope.

"Come on, gentlemen. This doesn't seem like a hard question. Must I ask again? Who owns the trailer with the tag registered through the state of Oklahoma?"

Doug stiffens. He feels his face flush from his rising blood pressure as he tries to maintain a calm demeanor before he answers, "I guess I do, but it is registered through a corporation."

"And the corporation's main purpose is?"

"It was incorporated as an all-inclusive conglomerate for ownership of this race horse," as Doug turns and points to Magic's stall.

"Very well. Thank you for that disclosure. But you can see how I find it most curious that the phone being held as evidence was purchased in Oklahoma, also. Would you like to elaborate on the mere coincidence of this?

Doug offers a fake smile, shrugs, and forces a laugh while he looks at JJ and concedes, "That is quite a coincidence."

DOUGLAS HARTLY

"The Undersheriff and Deputy just left not long ago, and Undersheriff Morris seems to have picked up on the ranch and a connection to Oklahoma after he noticed the Oklahoma tag on the trailer. He asked some very pointed questions, and we feel that he thinks we are involved, if not directly, then overtly."

"Why, Doug. What's the connection?"

"The phone was purchased in Oklahoma, but not Oklahoma City. So the tag and phone both being from Oklahoma led the Undersheriff down the trail to possibly connecting us in some way."

"You told him then about your Oklahoma connection?"

"No, because the phone wasn't purchased in Oklahoma City, which made this more perplexing, so we stayed quiet."

"Pete asks, "El Reno?"

"That would have been our guess also. But then he said, Enid and that they had contacted the Garfield County Sheriff's Office for assistance."

"Enid, I can't think of any connection to Enid," admits Pete.

OFFICE OF
DETECTIVE DANIEL DOBBINS
OKLAHOMA CITY POLICE DEPARTMENT

"This dual investigation between the Canadian County Sheriff's Office and us has just been expanded to add another agency.

"Who, Kingfisher County Sheriff?"

"Nope, isn't even in Oklahoma. It's Los Angeles County."

"As in California?"

"Yes. Seems as if the Bordillon family received a visit, also, but this time someone was home, and she was subdued while he looked around."

"What did he take?"

"That's it, Danny. Nothing taken that they can determine, but he went through the victim's purse and closets.

LA County caught a break as the assailant dropped his cell. Both phones were burners, and the other was turned off, so they couldn't ping it. But get this, the phones were purchased in Enid."

Danny prompts, "Let me take this call, and then you can finish bringing me up to speed. I know we are homicide, but this is peaking my interest."

Pete reasons, "I agree. We are detectives."

ROSIE REDMOND ROSEMAN

"Thanks for calling, sweetheart. I love you, too. I'll tell her."

"Tell me what?"

"He took the keys with their package to the lab just to see what they could do with them. He said his lab bunch is pretty thorough."

"Okay, that's fine with me," states Connie as she chuckles.

Rosie turns and asks, "What's so funny?"

"I guess I was waiting for you to take a jab at the lab, because you showed them up when they swept Ludlow's office."

"I know, right?" counters Rosie with a broad smile. "Pete also said California found out the phones were purchased in Oklahoma, but not Oklahoma City."

"So where, if not Oklahoma City?"

"Pete said Enid. I told him I couldn't think of any Enid connection," as Rosie turns Connie's direction.

Connie stares straight ahead as she states, "I can, Phillip Chapman."

Connie draws closer to Rosie as she can see Rosie is deep in thought and preoccupied writing on the pad in front of her.

First item was from the security camera about the suspect with a question mark beside expensive shoes.

Connie glances down the list which contains notes about Ben, Geri, Jake, and Keri. Rosie swiftly slashes through their names, and Connie guesses that means they are off her radar as Rosie writes "Phillip Chapman, Enid" in their place.

Rosie stops writing, looks up at Connie and then repositions the pad so Connie can have a better view.

Connie continues, and next is "cell phones", and then "coins" with multiple tick marks.

Connie gives Rosie a quick glance and sees that all-too-telling look in her eyes, and Connie states, "Okay, let's go get comfortable. Grab your coffee and head to the morning room or gallery. Your choice!"

UNDERSHERIFF LYNN MORRIS

Lynn opens his office door and looks for whoever is closest and says, "Roy, see if Dwayne is 10-8, and if so, have him 10-19 my office."

"He was, Lynn, and he's on his way in now."

"Thanks, Roy."

Roy with a slight hesitation, "Anything I can do?"

"No thanks, but...on second thought, yes you can. Check our records for a Douglas Hartly and see if you get anything. I'll have a second name for you after Dwayne gets here."

"What's up, Lynn?" Dwayne asks as Roy leaves the office.

Lynn yells, "Roy, hold up a minute."

"Dwayne, do you know what Paige's full name is?"

"Sure, Jeremiah Jason."

"Okay, Roy, check Jeremiah Jason Paige with an 'i' in Paige along with Hartly."

"Will do. You have a date of birth?"

"No. That's what I'm looking for. If we have no record, check DMV Oklahoma for 'Hartly', and California DMV for 'Paige' and get DOB's run them both NCIC."

"Okay."

"What's up?" Dwayne asks as he tries to get more information, because he has known JJ off and on during several stops at the Bordillon ranch. Each stop was not so much to see JJ, but an attempt to see

Amanda, and Dwayne never turned down an opportunity to accept a glass of tea on the porch with her.

Lynn swivels Dwayne's direction and relates, "I just had a conversation with a detective from the Oklahoma City Police Department requesting information on the Bordillon incident. Seems they have an interest in our investigation."

CONSTANCE LOUISE SINCLAIR

"Okay, let's have it. What's the first thing you have a question mark beside on your list?" Connie states as she enters the gallery where Rosie sits.

"Well, first is 'shoes', only because I wanted a chance to confirm my suspicion that the perp's shoes were Rag and Bone's high-tops and expensive."

Rosie glances at Connie who is making a strange face and asks, "What?"

Connie quips, "Nothing. I just find it interesting you are using Pete's lingo with 'perp' instead of intruder or even suspect."

Rosie chuckles and adds, "You know the meaning of the saying, 'when in Rome' don't you?"

"Yes, I do. Please continue, detective."

"Let's see. Okay, Phillip Chapman. Did you ever figure out what he initially called you for at LAX?"

"I haven't thought any more about it. But with the Enid connection, I might just make a trip to see him. I think he will find it curious, also," states Connie.

"Then, next is cell phones, but that will have to wait until Pete decides whether or not to contact LA County Sheriff's Office. Pete doesn't believe in coincidence, so he said he wants to see if the lab boys can find anything concrete that ties the two events together."

Rosie, with a pinched expression and narrowing eyes, whines, "Guess that can wait," showing a touch of annoyance.

"The last item and the biggest question in my mind is the coins. So far, you mentioned three, but how many more do you know of?"

"Well, to tell the truth, I only knew of one, and that was the one that Charles always carried in his pocket. As I said, I thought it was used when he played golf to spot his ball position. I guess it just got left in the bottom of my purse when the hospital gave me Charles' items."

"When you were in California with Amanda is the first time you knew about a second coin?"

"Yes, but Rosie, doesn't it make sense that there would be more than one in case of loss or even if Charles misplaced one?"

"I guess, and now there are three, though. I was hoping you could shed some light on the possible number of initial coins and their significance, especially since this last one was received in the mail and addressed to Charles. I'm with Pete on this, I don't believe in coincidence.

I would love to see all of them together when Pete brings Charles' keys back."

"Let me get mine," Connie says. "Should we mark them someway so they don't get jumbled?"

"No, Charles' will be on his keyring. Do you think Amanda would part with hers?" Rosie states as her curiosity grows, and her mind switches gears once again.

"I'm not certain, but I can ask."

Connie returns to the room, drops her purse in the chair and protests, "It's gone!"

Rosie, feeling an insatiable and uncontrollable need to know, quickly jumps to her feet and insists, "Call Amanda, now!"

Connie has a short, but informative, conversation with Amanda. Connie turns to Rosie. Their eyes meet as Connie gives the nod of confirmation.

Rosie turns, walks to the French doors, crosses her arms and looks past the gardens toward Oklahoma City. Her mind spins wildly in an attempt to work through her thoughts.

SINCLAIR OIL COMPANY

"Yes, these are Mr. Sinclair's keys. Someone was inquiring about them after his passing, but I told her he had lost them sometime before his death."

"The name of the lady asking?"

"I don't know if I even made note of it. Let me think."

Pete asks, "Could you tell me, specifically, what they open?"

"Let me get someone to help you, as the only one I recognize is the initial coin identifying these as Mr. Sinclair's."

CONSTANCE LOUISE SINCLAIR

"Rosie, I'm going to Enid to visit with Phillip. You want to come? I believe he will find this whole fiasco interesting, mainly because I was speaking with him while the intruder was behind me on his phone."

"Sure. I want to meet him, watch his behavior, and see what vibes he gives off."

"I'm certain Phillip can offer some helpful information. Hey, we can have lunch out. I miss having someone to share meals with."

THE OFFICE OF PHILLIP CHAPMAN

"Hello, Mrs. Sinclair."

"Hi, Charis. Is Mr. Chapman available?"

"Please be seated, and I'll let Mr. Chapman know you are here."

"Thanks, Charis."

Phillip, opening his door, says, "Connie, do come in."

"Hello, Phillip, and happy to see you, Joyce," as Connie hugs her and turns to Rosie.

"Phillip and Joyce, I would like you to meet my good friend, Rosie Roseman. Rosie, this is Phillip and Joyce Chapman."

"Nice to meet you."

"Won't you both join us for lunch?" Joyce asks as she shakes Rosie's hand.

Connie declines and continues, "We are here on a little fact finding mission and also to see what you think, Phillip. We have an episode to tell you about."

"You have me intrigued, I must admit. Is there a problem with the prototype?"

"No," Connie states. "There was an intruder at the estate a few weeks back and also at a friend's in California."

"Sorry to hear that, Connie. Were you home? I hope not."

"No. No one was home. Rosie and her husband, Pete, are house-sitting while I was away, and Pete came home early and saw evidence that someone had entered."

"Really," adds Joyce. "How frightening."

"I know, but luckily, Pete is a detective with the Oklahoma City Police Department, so appropriate action has been taken."

Phillip holds his breath at the declaration of Pete's position and employer.

"That's good," declares Joyce.

"Yes, but Phillip, the Los Angeles County Sheriff's Office have located a phone dropped by the assailant at the California ranch and has identified the phone's purchase location as Becky's Circle B Quick Stop."

"How curious," states Joyce. "Becky's here in Enid? I wonder what day? I get gas there all the time, and you do too, don't you, Phillip!"

Everyone looks to Phillip who is sitting unnaturally still as Connie picks up the dialogue and states, "Phillip, there's more. I think I met the intruder at the airport while I was on the phone with you."

"Really!"

"I heard him say, 'Yes, Boss."

Connie sees a slight quiver of Phillip's chin and continues, "Yes, when you called to offer me a lift home."

"Do tell."

"When was this, Phillip? A lift home from where? I don't remember that. Did you tell me about it?" Joyce inquires.

Phillip looks at Connie in an unblinking gaze, and as they make eye contact, Phillip sees the momentary waiver of Connie's eyes as she comes to a realization. The realization she was speaking to Rosie and not Phillip at the time she overheard the conversation.

Phillip stands, straightens the cuffs of his pristine shirt as he crosses the room, stopping at the floor to ceiling window.

Connie, with an uneasy chuckle, asks, “How did you even know I was in California? Did you speak with Geri?”

“California?” states Joyce.

No answer is forth coming as Connie continues, “You know, Ben and Geri Wilson, they are my neighbors.”

Rosie turns in her seat to get a view of Phillip’s face, but he has his back to her, so she strains to see his reflection, as she queries, “Why exactly did you contact Connie at LAX? It seems she can’t remember.”

Another gaping moment occurs as Phillip staunchly grasps silence.

Connie feels the burn of irritation flowing throughout. Her smile hardens while she stiffly stands.

Phillip turns from the window as he reads her change in character.

Then suddenly, Connie as she grabs Rosie’s arm in a quick pull, adds, “We have kept you from lunch long enough, haven’t we?” The ladies hastily leave Phillip and Joyce’s presence.

Joyce stands and exclaims, “But Connie, you didn’t give Phillip a chance to answer.”

ROSIE REDMOND ROSEMAN

"What the heck was that all about? You're thinking the same thing as I am. He had no answer for giving a reason why he called. But I wanted to give him a little time to say something, especially when you asked how he knew you were in California.

I wanted to read his body language, not just rush out. I saw the visible tension as his neck muscles twitched."

Connie says, "I wasn't on the phone with Phillip when the guy said, 'Yes Boss.' I hadn't spoken with Phillip yet. I was still talking with you before Phillip's call came and interrupted our conversation.

Something's up. I felt so, so exposed as it seemed he was looking at me, but also straight through me. I had to get out of there."

Connie looks back. Phillip is unmoved from the window.

PHILLIP CHAPMAN

"I did what you asked and got Connie to use my Citation so you could check her luggage, but you didn't tell me you had your goon right there with her.

What are you thinking? I told you about the conversation at the golf course when I overheard Charles on the phone. I didn't know, at the time, you would use it against them and to what manner? Connie is a dear friend. I feel responsible, and you put her in danger.

I feel like driving down there, but I'm too distraught, especially when Connie said the phones were bought in Enid. If you think you are going to shift the blame my direction, it won't work. What exactly are you trying to pull? What is it that Connie has that belongs to you, or does it?"

SINCLAIR OIL COMPANY

"Hello, Detective…?"

"Yes, I'm Detective Roseman, and you are?"

"I'm Anthony McGovern, Head of Security. I was told you have Mr. Sinclair's keys."

"Yes, they mysteriously were mailed to his widow at their home a few days ago."

"Really. Mr. Sinclair was upset when his keys were lost. May I see them? Yes, these are Mr. Sinclair's as this is his coin."

"What is the significance of the coin? Does every employee have them?"

"Everyone that has authorization to files and documents. In years past, these coins were used to obtain non-electronic, or as they are called, 'hard copies'. You would leave your coin upon acquisition of the document to identify who had the file, but not any longer."

"So the coins are no longer in use?"

"No, newer ones are still in use as each is encoded and can be placed on the terminal or computer to gain access, but only if you have the proper clearance. Each coin has different security levels."

Pete continues, "What level will this coin be able to access?"

"This coin is older and not encoded and is used for file copy access. We really felt that the keys would be returned a long time ago. It must be four or five years since these went missing."

"Mr. McGovern."

"Please, detective, call me Mac."

"I didn't mean to cut you off, but I noticed you changed your wording from lost to missing. Is there some significance in that?"

"Mr. Sinclair had initially thought he had left them in his desk drawer as he always did before a leisure activity, but afterwards he couldn't find them. He just assumed he had lost them on the golf course."

"Are all office doors and desks locked when they are not in use?"

"Usually, but no matter, because if these were received by mail, they were probably found and dropped in a mailbox where they would have been delivered to our service center."

Pete pushes on, "I need to know what these keys open, and also I want to know if there are any files that have one of Mr. Sinclair's coins connected with it."

"I'll have to check with someone in legal and get back with you as I'm not certain if a subpoena will be necessary. I'll have someone give you a call. Nice speaking with you and thanks for returning the keys."

"Oh, no, thank you, but the keys stay with me as they are part of an ongoing investigation, and I'll wait to see someone now. 'Mac', is it?"

ANTHONY MCGOVERN
Sinclair Security Officer

"Hey, there's a Detective Roseman from the Oklahoma City Police Department at reception, and he has Charles' keys. Someone else inquired about them several months back. Wasn't it that friend of yours?

ROSIE REDMOND ROSEMAN

"Pete, can you talk?" Rosie asks nervously.

"Yes, for a minute. I'm waiting for someone."

"Okay, this won't take long, I'll make it quick. Connie and I just left Phillip Chapman's Office."

"Who?"

"Oh, I'm not certain you know about…yes, you do. He's the one that contacted Connie and offered her a ride home from California."

"Okay, she was on the phone with him when the perp was behind her at LAX."

"Yes. That's him."

"So, why did you go to see him?"

"To run all this by him as his office is in Enid. There's something up with him."

"Do what? He's the burner phone connection, and you two did what? You went up there and gave him all our information. Do you know what you did? We have completely lost the element of surprise when we talk with him. Oh, Rosie!"

ANNA MILLER
Sinclair Oil

"Hello, Detective Roseman. I'm Anna Miller, and I hear you have recovered Charles' keys."

"Yes, and I am interested in what these keys go to and the significance of files that Mr. Sinclair had used his coin to obtain."

"May I see them? Thank you. Please follow me."

She stops at the office denoted as "Charles Sinclair, Chief Executive Officer" and uses one of the keys to open the door.

Pete follows her and sees the over-sized executive desk, credenza with glass shelving on both sides filled with memorabilia and adjacent file cabinets.

"I can identify a few more of the keys as this is his desk key, this is the credenza key, and these smaller ones are his file cabinet keys."

As Pete retrieves the keys, he adds, "So that leaves his initial coin and two keys."

"I would think that they could be his keys for use at his residence."

Pete adds as he checks his notes. "Do you know what files Mr. Sinclair's coin references, and has his office been left undisturbed since Mr. Sinclair's passing?"

"No, not by any means. Files and papers were sorted and incorporated into the appropriate areas of business concern whether obtained through use of his coin or preliminary customer consultation. Everything else is just the same, all the pictures, plaques, awards, and certificates."

"Mrs. Sinclair didn't visit and retrieve any items?"

"Not that I'm aware of."

"Thank you, Miss Miller. You have been very helpful. Can you think of anything else that could help me in this matter?" states Pete as he flips the keys in his hand hoping to see if she knew who had asked previously for them.

"No. I can think of nothing."

"Okay, thank you."

"Certainly, I am more than happy to help. Let me show you out."

Pete follows her toward the front entrance, and as he glances at the floor he positions himself to note her every reaction as he remarks, "Oh, one more question!"

"Yes."

"Who else inquired about the missing keys?"

With a slight flutter of her eyes but maintaining an even tone, she states, "Deidra Hulbert from Driscoll and Driscoll Law Firm."

PETER ROSEMAN

Seated in his car, Pete thinks, *why didn't Anna Miller offer info on Hulbert when I asked if she could think of anything more?* He writes beside Anna Miller's name, 'Suspected deception'.

SINCLAIR ESTATE

"Hello, ladies," Pete hollers. "I know you are home, but where?"

"Pete, honey, we're in the gallery."

"Okay. Here you are." Pete groans almost in a hoarse voice from yelling.

Rosie, with a peck on the cheek, greets her husband and silently thinks, *I'm ready to go home and back to our life. Our life as a couple,* but comments, "Have you had a productive day? I, or we, want to apologize for not checking with you before we went to Enid and met with Phillip Chapman."

"Yes, Pete, I never dreamed that I would leave Phillip and Joyce with the feeling of dismay and underlying distrust," states Connie. "Rosie said we made you lose the element of surprise."

"It puts the investigation in an awkward position, and we will just have to approach it from a different direction. I will deal with that later. Now, Connie, I want you to look at these keys once more."

"Okay, what am I looking at?"

"I visited Sinclair Oil today and spoke with Anna Miller. What is her position with the company?"

"She is Charles' secretary, but they don't use that term any longer. Her official title is Executive Administrative Assistant."

"Well, Miss Miller helped to establish the use of all the keys except these two. Al, in the Lab, believes this one is a bank key, possibly safety deposit but this larger one, no idea."

Connie offers, "That's possible."

Pete takes a seat and continues, "I can check with Miss Miller as to the bank Sinclair Oil utilizes for business, but I'm not entirely convinced as to Miss Miller's total and complete disclosure of facts and even to her statement that she doesn't know what the last two keys open. How well do you know her?"

Connie, without hesitation, remarks, "Not well at all. Lucy Carmichael retired several years ago, and there have been a few since then. It seems each would use her new title and position as a stepping stone for advancement to bigger oil companies."

Pete slides the keys across the glass top coffee table and states, "The two other keys are the ones in question, and I'm wondering if these open a safety deposit at the company's bank. Which bank would that be?"

Connie catches the keys as they slide from the side of the table and advises, "Sinclair Oil's business account is at BancFirst, but our household account along with our joint account is at MidFirst, El Reno."

"Are these trust accounts?"

"Well, yes they are. What significance is that?"

"So they were set up by your law firm?"

"The accounts weren't created by the firm but the trust was, and everything is tied to the trust.

The BancFirst account is in the corporation's name, Sinclair Oil, LLC."

DETECTIVE PETER ROSEMAN

"Danny, I know I'm spending a lot of time on this case and thanks for covering me on that last assignment we caught, but I think I'm getting close to pulling this thing together."

"So you have a lead on the intruder?"

"No, but Charles keeps dropping us clues that send me down a trail that never seems to be a dead end."

"You talking about the keys?"

"Yes, either there is a plant at Sinclair Oil, or someone there is in cahoots with the law firm's investigator. It seems Investigator Deidra Hulbert was asking about the keys after Charles death, and Anna Miller didn't disclose this information until I pointedly ask her."

"Have you contacted Enid's Police Department about the burn phones? I know your wife and Mrs. Sinclair went to Enid and spoke with Mrs. Sinclair's friend, and you were a little concerned about that, but we couldn't investigate in their city without first asking their assistance."

"No, I haven't. At first, I was upset over their meeting with Phillip Chapman, and the outcome, none the less, was productive in obtaining information that is pertinent, but if this thing ends up in court, they will have to testify."

"Maybe you should bring that little nugget to their attention and give them something to consider before heading out on their own in the future."

"You may be right, but I'll hold off on getting Rosie and Connie on the defensive, because we may have to ask them to get in an advantageous position in the law firm. Driscoll's investigator may have had a directive to inquire about the keys or she might be with Anna Miller in some way. Either way, Driscoll and Driscoll are not going to roll over easily, even if we can connect them."

CONSTANCE LOUISE SINCLAIR

"We're here. MidFirst Bank."

Pete stops after exiting the car and asks, "What is that?"

"What?" repeats Connie.

"I smell it too," exclaims Rosie.

Connie with a wide smile and a chuckle, proclaims, "Welcome to El Reno, the home of the onion fried hamburger and much, much more. You are in for a treat as lunch is on me. If we are done before two, we will eat at Jobe's Drive-In. My stomach is so ready for a charburger with cheese and onion rings."

"Well, let's get this done."

"Hello, may I help you?" comes from a smiling face as soon as they enter the lobby area.

"Yes, I'm Constance Sinclair, and I would like to see if one of these keys are to a safety deposit box or drawer."

"I'll get someone to assist you with that. Please be seated."

Rosie and Connie take a seat, but Danny remains standing with his back to the wall where he has a full view of all areas of the lobby as Rosie professes, "We should have come here first, but I was certain the keys would open something at the oil company's bank."

Connie, with a pat to her hand, warns, "We're not certain either will work here."

"Mrs. Sinclair, I'm Vonna Mason. Would you join me in my office?"

"Certainly," replies Connie as all three sit.

"Do you know your account number that this drawer is associated with so I can pull it up?"

"Well, it's one of two. I'm guessing our personal account, and the number is 2626222793. If that's not correct, it will be our household account."

"Yes, I found it, and you and Mr. Sinclair are both signatories on the account."

"Charles passed some time back."

"Oh, I'm sorry. My condolences."

"Thank you so much, Miss Mason."

"Mrs. Sinclair, you should consider updating. We will need a certified copy of the death certificate, and it would be wise to have two signatures on each account, also."

"Thanks, I'll consider that at a later date."

"Let's see. Yes, it has a drawer associated with it. Do you have your key in your possession?"

"Yes, I do. It is one of these two."

After turning both keys in her hand, Miss Mason announces, "How strange."

Pete asks, "Strange? In what way?"

Miss Mason continues, "The key that is engraved 'MF' and also marked 'do not copy' is ours but this one that is marked with 'OK' could be to the bank previously at this location."

"And that would be?" queries Pete.

"OK Federal, Oklahoma Federal Savings and Loan, but the key appears to be too large."

Miss Mason returns the keys to Connie and states, "I'll need to see two forms of ID."

Connie complies, but her attention is on Pete as she notices his nod in her direction.

Miss Mason scans the cards into the computer, and Pete continues, "Is Mrs. Sinclair's identification being attached to this account?"

"Here you go, you can have these back. And yes, these are assigned as a virtual fingerprint identifying file activity. This augments and enhances every interaction taken. We are in the process of updating our capabilities to computer generate a photo to record each transaction which will also be pertinent."

"How would this information be obtained? Could Mrs. Sinclair obtain a copy now?"

"No, I'm afraid not. Mrs. Sinclair and her husband own the accounts, but documentation of access is part of our security that the bank uses to maintain the trust and integrity we are known for. Do you have any further questions?"

Pete adds, "Just one more. Is your bank in possession of the box the OK Federal key opens?"

"My first instinct is to tell you certainly not," discloses Miss Mason, "as I know that key should have been surrendered with OK Federal's closure and also the size difference between keys.

The drawer is placed on the counter, and Miss Mason advises, "Let me know when you're through."

After Miss Mason departs, Connie maneuvers the long rectangular lid and lays it to the side only to be met by a loud gasp from Rosie. Pete steps forward and lifts two thick files encased in blue binders signifying legal documents, but Rosie is honed in on the source of her derision. Connie backs two steps back as Rosie lifts from the drawer Charles' initial coin.

JOBE'S DRIVE IN

While comfortably seated at Jobe's, Peter states, "I'm hungry, and you're certain this is good?"

"What could I get you, folks?"

"Hello, Dorothy," replies Connie. "These are my friends, Pete and Rosie, and I'm introducing them to the wonderful world of hamburgers and coney's. Who's cooking? Robert or Charlie?"

"It's Charlie today," as Connie gives a wave to the pickup window.

"I want a charburger with cheese and rings," Connie enthusiastically states.

"Pete, you have to have the chicken fry. It is the best ever or the Indian Taco."

Pete asserts, "You talked me into it. Chicken fry it is."

Rosie comments, "Indian Taco, please. I've never had one, except at the fair."

"Well, get ready to move this one up several notches above the fair," adds Connie.

"And your drinks?" asks Dorothy.

"Tea all around," as each nods.

Connie rambles, "You can get a root beer float here, and when Charles and I were dating, I always had a cherry vanilla Dr. Pepper. Of course, in the car, as this was, and still is, a kid's hangout. They would put different animals on your straws, and Charles' car had them on the sun visors and anywhere they would fit. Fond memories."

“This is really a neat place. Look at all the Coke memorabilia, and what is that article about?”

“That’s an article on ‘Cowboy’ Bill Feddersen and his world renowned Rodeo career. Bill was so good at bull riding that he was among the top 15 competitors in the world and has been inducted into the National Cowboy Hall of Fame,” proudly states Connie.

“This town is so unique, not only for having a downtown but Burger Day the first weekend in May and Small Town Weekend the first weekend in June. I could go on and on. Cocobellas, Sid’s, Robert’s, Johnnies, Blue 99, Iron Tree Coffee, Our Glass Wine Bistro, and there is even a quilt shop, with not only quilts but fabric and lessons. Our newest is a boutique called Wandering Daisy. Oh my, and the music history, we even have a producer. Then there’s historic Ft. Reno, and we are the only town to have a railed trolley that you can ride through the downtown area. Charles was on the city council for a short time, and El Reno Capital Improvement projects were his passion. ”

“Here’s our food, so let’s enjoy a meal together, my dear friends.”

PETER ROSEMAN

Back at the estate, Pete asks some pointed questions, "So you weren't aware of the box before today?"

"No, never, I feel so foolish. I knew there was one, now that I think about it, but it never came to mind, not once, and a definite no on two drawers," states Connie.

"A better question is why, during the asset sale of your property, your legal representation didn't at least check deeds and abstracts?"

Rosie rolls the coin around between her fingers and quietly thinks of any and all ramifications this fourth one might divulge. She examines the back of the coin as Pete explains its significance and thinks each coin needs to be compared.

Pete continues, "Okay. I'm at a loss here. We have the abstract to this estate made out in the Sinclair Trust name and also an abstract to a California property made out to Jessie Sinclair. I have access to all kinds of forensic people, but I don't have anyone to tell me what this means."

Connie notes, "I can help a little. The Sinclair Revocable Trust is supposed to cover any and all property in our possession and gives the trustees authority to buy, sell, convey, etc. anything covered by the trust."

"So the trust is now in your name since Charles has passed?"

"Oh Pete, you are pushing me beyond my knowledge," Connie confesses."

"Who is Jessie Sinclair, and is this the deed to the Bordillon Ranch?"

Rosie, still rolling the coin, adds, "And a fourth coin."

LOS ANGELES COUNTY SHERIFF'S DEPARTMENT

"Lynn, it's up to you. I just know him from stopping by occasionally at the ranch, and I have had no reason to think him anything but an upstanding ranch owner," mumbles Dwayne.

"He owns the Bordillon ranch and not the girl?"

"I was just under that assumption. Guess we could check the assessor's records to be certain."

"Dwayne, after Roy gave me the info from NCIC on that murder case in Oklahoma showing Paige being detained as a material witness and, on top of that, both the victim and defendant lived and worked in Los Angeles County, I feel we have just cause to at least question him further."

"Hartly came back clean, and he is the owner of the Oklahoma tagged horse hauler, not JJ."

"That's my point. If it had ended with no record on Hartly, then there would be no connection to Paige and Oklahoma, but now Hartly's clear but Paige has been pulled in with an Oklahoma link and not such a clean one on top of that.

The whole area is up in arms over the unsolved home invasion, and I'm not waiting long. The Sheriff is not happy either with reelection looming, and if Paige is involved, let's get to the bottom of this and be done.

Check the courthouse for ownership of that land. I'll wait that long."

CONSTANCE SINCLAIR

"Yes, this is Constance Sinclair, and I was wondering when Arthur or Matthew might be available to speak with me?"

"Let me check, Mrs. Sinclair. May I ask what this is concerning?"

"Title to property."

"Okay, I'll block you in for an hour, and the next available will be a week from tomorrow. Would ten be convenient for you?"

"Yes, that will be fine."

"I've got you, Mrs. Sinclair, for Thursday, the thirteenth at 10 A.M. Is there anything else I may help you with?

"Who will I be seeing?"

"Your consultation will be with Arthur Driscoll."

ROSIE REDMOND ROSEMAN

"Connie, you mean we have a whole week until we can get verification to what this all means. That's a little disturbing."

"I know, I'm right with you. It seems like we are at a standstill, and to top it off, Pete has been pulled to help Danny on a homicide. At least, we can be grateful we're not in the middle of that."

Rosie with a heavy sigh, moans, "Yes, I guess."

"Rosie, let's just take a break. Give your mind a rest."

"I wish," insists Rosie with brows knitted.

Connie exclaims, "I know, do you want to go to the mall? Doesn't have to be Penn Square. We can go up to Quail Springs, your choice."

Rosie gives no answer, and Connie suddenly jumps to her feet and adds, "Williams-Sonoma. We can get a mandolin, and they have all kinds of jams and jellies."

Rosie, with purpose insists, "Where's that pad with my list? I need to add this fourth coin and possible second key to OK Federal. We know the intruder was looking for the coins, but the two he has might not open what he needs."

Rosie finds it difficult to commit to anything, as she tries to make sense of the current situation, and rampant thoughts race through her head. She feels the inability to relax or even smile has been replaced by her feelings of what lies ahead.

PETER ROSEMAN

"Sorry, Danny. That was Rosie."

"What did she say, anything wrong?"

"No, she wants me to bring Charles' keys home tonight. I told her it looks like a long evening since we are in the middle of this homicide, so she and Connie are on their way to retrieve them," Pete states as he shakes his head in apparent bewilderment.

"Pete, what is it?"

"Danny, I think Rosie is in full 'mind' mode over this whole thing. That can't be good."

CONSTANCE LOUISE SINCLAIR

"I'll wait in the car while you run in and get the keys."

"Connie, come on in."

"No, I'm good here."

"I don't think it will take long if Pete's in his office."

"I'm okay waiting here. The last time I was in those offices was when we got tossed in jail. I don't want to resurrect that memory again."

"I won't be long. I just need to get all the pieces back in front of me, along with our list we have, and see what turns up."

Rosie, as promised, quickly returns to the car.

"Wow, that wasn't long. So now can we hit a few stores?" questions Connie enthusiastically."

"Okay," states Rosie slowly.

"Let's run through Williams-Sonoma and find something to inspire me to cook since there are three of us. It's difficult to enjoy cooking for one."

The drive was quiet as Rosie seems uneasy.

Connie chatters on. "They have all kinds of jams and jellies and yeast. Yes, I'll get some yeast and make bread. I used to make it all the time, Italian Rosemary and Jewish Challah bread which is braided and soooo good."

Rosie suddenly comes to life. "Isn't the law firm close to the store?"

"Well, yes, we just passed it. It's in Founders Tower. Oh, what a view."

Rosie in a rushed voice instructs, "Quick, get in the right lane and take May Avenue exit. We can get there off of May."

Connie obediently follows directions and informs, "But my appointment is a week from now."

Rosie is miraculously revived. Her energy is intense as she straightens, takes control of the situation and directs the next couple of turns ending at the tower with the final order. "Park here, and let's think."

"Let's think. So now you include me."

Pete said that that secretary at Sinclair Oil…"

Connie quickly corrects with, "Executive Administrative Assistant."

Rosie, not missing a beat, rebuffs, "As I was saying, that secretary told Pete that Deidra Hulbert was also asking for these keys."

"You haven't put those away yet. You could lose them."

"Connie, turn around here and listen," Rosie declares as she continues to search her mind for words that will convey what needs to be done."

Connie unbuckles and shifts in the seat of her white Lexus, giving her full attention to the Rosie she remembers so distinctly when she is rolling things around in her mind.

Rosie sits for a moment as uncertainty and a little self-doubt grasp her, but that moment is fleeting as her delayed response turns to a hesitant nod.

"You know that Hulbert woman well enough to casually drop by? Can you think of any reason to get us in to see her?"

Connie's only reply is a shy non-committal answer of, "Maybe," while she leans away from Rosie to get a full view of her face.

Connie sees Rosie's rising determination as Connie remarks, "Let's put this on the back burner for now, okay?"

"No, Connie. We need to get in there, and while you talk, I can see Hulbert's reaction to the keys."

"You're going to toss them in your hand or something?"

"Exactly. But right now it's or 'something'," Rosie quips with growing resolve.

Connie weakly agrees while showing her half-hearted support and answers, "Give me a little bit to think this through."

"You can think on the way. Come on."

Connie feels frustration tinged with a small amount of anger as she thinks Rosie is too quickly dismissing the ramification of what might transpire.

Connie diligently tries to delay and requests more time, but all she receives is Rosie's passive roll of the eyes and then her aggressive push toward the entrance door.

Connie thinks as they enter the elevator, *"Oh Lord, I pray for your protection and please get us through this."*

Rosie eagerly moves Connie further in the elevator as Connie replies, "Slow down. How are we going to get past the front desk if I don't have a reasonable explanation?"

Just then the doors open, and Connie is frozen in place as Rosie gushes, "Come on, dear. That was a short ride. We're here."

Connie feels tremors in her hands and fingers as she reluctantly exits, fearing she has broken out in a profuse sweat.

Rosie stops quickly, and Connie almost runs into her. Rosie spins around to check for anyone coming from the other direction and cautiously adds, "The receptionist is not here, but I think she is coming from the far end of the hall. Do you know what to ask when she gets back to her desk?"

As they hear the heels advancing on the marble entry, Connie and Rosie turn at the sound of, "Mrs. Sinclair. Good to see you again. Are you ladies going down or just arriving?"

Connie, with regained composure, states in a subdued tone, "It's her."

Then answers, "Oh, Miss Hulbert, we're going down."

Rosie, in disbelief tries to rescue the situation and save face, adds, "Oh yes. Let me find the keys." Taking Charles' keys, she interjects, "Connie hold these while I find the car keys."

Rosie steps back to see Hulbert's non-reaction as Connie moves the keys in an obvious manner from hand to hand and declares, "Oh, yes, Charles' keys. Thank you."

Rosie insists, "No problem. Miss Hulbert, we'll ride down with you."

Deidra Hulbert presses the button while she turns and relates to two women coming into view several feet away, "I'll be out the rest of the day."

One answers, "I'll hold your calls, so please be sure to check back."

Deidra Hulbert steps into the elevator and uses her hand to restrain the doors.

The second lady straightens and purposefully heads towards Connie in a hastened walk and uncertainty on her face. She abruptly stops and questions, "Mrs. Sinclair, what are you doing here? How did you know to come?"

Deidra already has her hand on her phone that rests in the side pocket of her purse while she says goodbye and lets the doors close.

Connie is dumb founded, but Rosie jumps in, "We were just speaking with Mrs. Hulbert," and added nothing more.

Connie thinks, *"Thank you, Lord! I'm grateful Rosie is a quick thinker and truthful as we certainly were speaking with Miss Hulbert."*

"Well, when you get home, there will be a message that Mr. Driscoll would like to see you at your earliest convenience."

"You've had a cancellation to Arthur's calendar? That's wonderful, but I'm not prepared to see him now as I don't have the documents in question with me."

"Oh, it's not Arthur Driscoll. It's Matthew."

Connie is quiet but thinks, *Really, Matthew is the quiet one and never seems to have much input.*

"Step this way, and I'll see if this is concerning your appointment with Arthur."

ARTHUR DRISCOLL

Arthur enters Matthews's office in a troubled manner. He assumes a strained smile as he sees Matthew's new hire. Matthew has pressured him into hiring a new investigator, even though they have a very capable one in Deidra Hulbert.

Arthur takes several deep breaths to calm himself and implores, "I didn't mean to enter unannounced. I didn't realize you had someone with you."

Matthew, with a swift glance, exclaims, "Thank you. We can continue later."

Arthur thinks it strange that he exits through the back entrance that he and Matthew use to leave the building without being noticed.

Arthur's passing thought is pushed aside as his focus returns to the problem at hand.

"Matthew, several files have been altered in the electronic copies. I have asked to have the original files located to see if it can be determined what has been changed."

Matthew coughs to try and maintain his composure and lower his rising blood pressure as his heart beats at an accelerated rate, and adds, "Well, I must admit that is strange. Strange indeed."

Arthur continues, "IT personnel are attempting to locate the IP address when the files were last accessed. This will tell us what computer was used and the exact time and date of entry. If we have been hacked, we need to figure it out quickly."

ROSIE REDMOND ROSEMAN

"What is taking so long? She went to ask a simple question. I learned what I needed to know as Deidra Hulbert didn't notice Charles' keys. Let's get out of here. Make some excuse. Surely you have a pressing need that must be attended to."

Connie, feeling a little exasperated, implores, "Can't you enjoy this beautiful building built in a sphere? If we continue to walk this outer hall, it will give us a 360-degree view of Oklahoma City."

Rosie admits, "I guess because I wasn't paying any attention, and I don't even think I can lead us out."

Connie gives a minimal response and then goes silent as she deals with her frustration that often happens between the two friends.

Connie throws her hands up in an "I give up" gesture and quips, "Come on. We will take the scenic route back to the elevators."

Rosie thinks, *"Oh Lord, I'm sorry, but my mind seems to be on problem solving, and I need my list and quiet time."*

Through gritted teeth, while she briefly closes her eyes and takes a deep breath, instructs, "At least gaze to your left and just marvel at the view."

MATTHEW DRISCOLL'S SECRETARY
Aka Executive Administrative Assistant!

"Matthew, Mrs.…Oh, Mr. Driscoll, I didn't realize you were in conference. I'll give you a moment."

"Not necessary, Julie," answers Arthur. "I was just leaving."

Matthew, to further silence his assistant, raises a hand until his office door is secure. Even then, he waits several seconds before allowing her to speak.

"I was going to tell you, Mrs. Sinclair is here and I thought you might want to see her."

Matthew runs his hand over his face to help disguise his emotion. Three close encounters were about all he could handle. First Phillip's continual calls, then Arthur walks in while he is in a conversation over the next decision to be made in the ongoing surveillance, and now his assistant discloses Mrs. Sinclair's presence.

"Matthew?"

"Yes, what?"

Matthew shows more of his discomfort than he likes before he notes, "No, now is not the time."

CONSTANCE LOUISE SINCLAIR

Rosie listens as Connie rambles on while pointing in the distance and proclaiming every church, hospital and even her favorite place to have her oil changed.

Rosie is vexed beyond belief by the unresolved problems and is feeling hindered in her efforts to complete the synopsis knocking at the door of her mind. She lackadaisically makes herself obediently walk the circle and engage in the vista view it provides. She suddenly feels ashamed of her pleadings and inability to relax as Connie's free spirit chatters on.

Rosie thinks, *I might as well have flung myself on the floor in a childish tantrum, yet again!*

Rosie feels her guilt continue to manifest itself and is immediately convicted by her emotions, but as she turns from the window to acknowledge her transgressions and apologize to Connie, she is distracted by the man ahead walking hastily to a side door.

Could it be?

Rosie pushes past Connie, leaving Connie a gasp.

Connie gives pursuit through the door and finds Rosie with eyes focused on the digital monitor as it reveals the slow progression of descending numbers.

Connie stops behind Rosie, feels the flush of embarrassment creep across her cheeks from the lack of composure the two ladies had ignored by running full gait through the halls of the law firm. Connie thinks, Lord *help us, so much for decency and order.*

Rosie turns with eyes wide as she glances back to the bank of elevators and is almost at a loss for words, if that's possible. She stands with an unfocused gaze and rebuffs, "Are you kidding? That was him!"

Connie turns her head and lowers herself to capture Rosie's attention and grasp the significance of the moment.

Connie, with a shake of the head, queries, "You're saying you saw the intruder? Impossible!"

JEREMIAH JASON PAIGE

"Pete, what did the video show from the convenience store in Enid? Did it match the security footage at Connie's?"

"No, sorry, JJ."

"It didn't match or wasn't enough to tell?"

"Neither, I haven't obtained a copy or much less know if they have obtained one."

"Pete, Amanda needs some closure. What seems to be the problem?"

Pete's mind races as he is caught in the middle of this bizarre drama. Where precisely does the Bordillon family fit now? Could the abstract to the California property be to their ranch, and if so, what are the implications? JJ professes love for Connie, but if he has to choose between Amanda and Connie, who will he choose?

"Pete, you still there?"

Pete's thought process quickens faster than his mind's comprehension, and the only thing he can think to do, either right or wrong, is stall.

"JJ, I'm on it and I'll get back to you."

ROSIE REDMOND ROSEMAN

"What time is it?"

Connie looks at the dash and instructs, "Almost noon. The clock is right there."

"Where?"

"Right there. You can tell time on a conventional clock, can't you?"

Rosie, in a tone of disbelief, adds, "This fancy car, and it doesn't have a digital clock?"

"Well, no!" quips Connie, "So you go right ahead and ask the time whenever you feel the need. How many times are we going to drive around this building, anyway?"

"I was in hopes Mr. No Good would still be in the area, and we could get a description and tag number for Pete to put out an APB."

"Put out a what?"

"You know, don't you watch *48 Hours*? An APB, all-points bulletin."

"Guess I'd better add that to the DVR list," Connie quips.

Rosie counters, "Just head home, I want to compare this coin with the one we got from the bank."

Connie feels a little anger and shock at Rosie's defensive attitude and tries to defuse the situation by stating, "We're just hungry. It's noon. Let's stop at Bravo's for lunch? Italian and on me!"

"Oh no, only if we can get it to-go. We need to stay on the move."

DETECTIVE DANIEL DOBBINS

"ME says Bell died from the gunshot wound before the accelerant was applied. We need to determine which of the suspects shot her and set the car on fire, and if both are culpable," Danny states as he walks the familiar route around his office he uses to clarify facts and bring details into perspective.

"Pete, check your notes, and see when the neighbors called 911."

"Oh, it was 10:43 P.M." Pete answers as he brings his mind back to his job and off of his conversation with JJ.

"And when did dispatch get the call of the car fire?"

"Pete, you did talk with the first responders, didn't you?"

Pete flips through his notes, but it is evident that Pete hasn't made the call.

Danny comes to a halt as his focus remains on Pete. Danny's mind pushes him in the direction that Pete is predisposed, with thoughts of the call he had stepped in the hall to answer, and Danny openly challenges Pete.

"What is going on with you?" Danny asks in a passively controlled query.

Pete keeps his eyes on his notes as he continues to scan the page.

"Is there a problem we need to talk about so that we can get back to the case?"

Pete slowly considers his options in telling Danny anything, and if so, how much, as he adds, "It's just this California deal and the intruder."

Danny opens his mouth to interject something and then thinks better and takes a deep breath. His frustration was quickly heightening, and his controlled behavior had advanced to anger.

"Pete, you know I am your friend, but at the same time, I am your superior," as Danny hastily slaps the file on his desk.

"Our job is homicide and not breaking and entering. This is partly my fault as I encouraged you to pursue aggressively the leads at first, but we have a case now, and you need…No, I am telling you, I expect your full attention to be turned back to this department and this case. Are we at an understanding?"

ROSIE REDMOND ROSEMAN

Rosie has stuck to her determination to get home and is on the phone to Pete.

Connie, with a defeated attitude, eyes the Schlotzsky's take-out at Rosie's feet.

"That's strange."

Connie remains silent.

"Pete's not answering," Rosie states as flawed images flash through her mind.

Connie feels regret at her desire to cold-shoulder Rosie, and continues, "It's lunch time. I bet it's too noisy for him to hear.'

"No, it's always in his pocket," Rosie relates as she mentally berates herself for her over-reaction to Pete not answering.

Connie asks, "Who are you calling now?"

"The main number to the police department," and then, "Hello, this is Peter Roseman's wife, could you connect me to his office?"

A few moments silence before, "There's no answer, but the board shows he is in the building. Could I page him for you?"

CONSTANCE LOUISE SINCLAIR

"Are you okay?"

"Oh, I feel better. At least, Pete found a moment to text me and tell me he couldn't talk, and it will be another long night."

"A long night again??? He already knows this early in the day that he's working late," Connie exclaims, as she thinks of the consequences of placing undue stress on Pete and Rosie's marriage.

Rosie perceives Connie's statement as dishonesty on Pete's part but chooses not to react.

As she drives them down NW Highway, Connie thinks back and knows she never had an inkling of Charles' dishonesty in their marriage when Charles would have to be gone weeks at a time. But, unfortunately, she now knows, she very well should have been more diligent.

Why, Lord? Why did I feel the need to bend to Charles' will in the past and now, still genuflecting to this very day?

ROSIE REDMOND ROSEMAN

Connie is first out of the car, and Rosie isn't sure if the door is an intentional slam, but as she enters the kitchen, wagging the Schlotzsky's take-out boxes and coming precariously close to dropping the drinks, she sees Connie rubbing the back of her neck with a damp cloth.

A tinge of shame comes over her as she sees her friend with both hands on the kitchen sink and head lowered. Rosie feels guilty, but along with the guilt, comes a generous sprinkling of denial of any wrong-doing on her part.

Gradually, Rosie concludes that she might have let her feelings take a little more control than appropriate.

Finally, Rosie admits, "Connie, I need to apologize. I'm just upset that we lost that guy at Driscoll's, and I wanted to ask Pete when we would see the security tapes from Enid. Now, more than ever, I need to see them while his image is fresh in my mind."

Connie listens as Rosie sees the slow up and down nod from Connie.

"And with Pete sleeping at our apartment in the city when he knows he will only get a few hours rest, it just makes everything more difficult."

Connie walks to the table, crumples upon the chair and seems distracted. Connie senses the rise of aversion, quickly prays the feelings will pass as she continues in silence.

Connie feels the need to stall, to give herself time to turn back the words that are forming with every breath. She knows that if she lets the discourse spill forth, that once spoken, it can never be retrieved. It would only advance and contribute to a strained relationship for which she's not prepared, and must avoid, at all cost.

Connie pushes words from her mind as she brings herself to acknowledge Rosie has been here, through thick and thin and back.

Connie answers, "My sweet friend. You owe me no apology. It just seems like you see clues, and I feel danger. You see a trail to follow, and I feel reluctance. Your mind comes up with logical conclusions, and mine sees the worst-case scenario. I just want some semblance of normalcy."

Rosie turns, and as their eyes meet, Connie walks toward her friend and states in a critical tone, "But I can tell you one thing, if this food is cold, this whole apology thing will have to be revisited!"

CONSTANCE LOUISE SINCLAIR

Connie, eyes widening, shakes her head as her phone rings.

Rosie grabs her napkins as she finishes her last bite and jumps to her feet.

Connie instantly holds her phone at a distance as the caller ID flashes. Rosie sees the disbelief on Connie's face as Connie shakes her head and drops the phone to the table.

Rosie races to retrieve it but has the same reaction as she places it back and both watch as the ringing continues. They look at each other as the phone precariously moves to the edge and Connie pushes Rosie to save it from a downward spiral culminating on the floor.

PHILLIP CHAPMAN

Phillip waits for the beep and begins, "Connie, this is Phillip. Sorry I missed you. I want to apologize for our unsettling conversation the last we met. Please call at your earliest convenience."

CONSTANCE LOUISE SINCLAIR

"Hello, JJ. What's up?"

"Connie, I spoke with Pete earlier today, and he said the security footage in Enid had not been reviewed."

"What time did you speak with him?"

"Well, eight here, so ten there."

"Rosie tried to call around noon, and he didn't pick up but texted that he couldn't talk. We know that they are working an arson-homicide and guessing that's what's going on," Connie replies.

"Doug and I have talked it over and we feel that this whole thing has ground to a halt, which is very disturbing."

"What is the sheriff telling you?" Connie asks at Rosie's urging.

"We haven't heard from him."

"Why didn't you call the sheriff after you weren't satisfied with Pete's answer?"

"Didn't Pete tell you what the undersheriff insinuated about the Oklahoma tag?"

"Yes, so?"

JJ feels the dryness in his mouth. His mind scrambles to come up with something that would diffuse the direction the conversation is going as he interjects, "Well, Doug and I didn't feel comfortable in calling. We thought we might catch Dwayne out on patrol and casually inquire."

JJ instantly regrets bringing Doug's name up but tries to gain a little distance by not leaving this a one-on-one conversation. JJ needs to slant the situation as he hurries to rearrange his thoughts and find a defense for the reprisal Connie undoubtedly is to unleash.

"J," Connie offers in a softened voice. "I don't seem to understand. The trailer is tagged in Doug's name, so why do I hear a reluctance on your part to speak to law enforcement?"

JJ remains silent as Connie continues, as if not expecting an answer.

"What is this…this insecurity, or is it lack of confidence in someone in authority? I know you don't have anything of consequence in your past such as an outstanding legal obligation, or you wouldn't have been released from jail here in Oklahoma.

You seem to have a flight response at any encounter or thought of meeting with law enforcement."

Connie's thoughts dredge up past history she has sworn never to revisit! Yes, the memory of JJ leaving for California while she remained in jail.

Why is she letting herself go there?

JEREMIAH JASON PAIGE

It was a brief conversation, but why can't I shake the feeling that Connie knows. She couldn't; no one does.

ROSIE REDMOND ROSEMAN

"You stayed unusually calm, especially after freaking out when Phillip Chapman called."

Connie smiles and admits, "I did, didn't I? Often, it seems JJ has a childlike need."

"Need for what?"

"I don't know. I haven't figured that out," states Connie, and then in a slow voice adds, "You don't think he has a fear of authority?"

Rosie, lets a deep breath escape as she feels the unresolved problems in her equation being hindered. "Really, what could have brought that on?"

Connie thinks, *Who knows?* She turns to Rosie, "Okay, my friend, I might not know J's needs, but I definitely know yours, and if I have learned nothing else, it's your dogged persistence to find answers or at least rehash the information you have over and over."

"We need to see that footage," Rosie declares.

"Well, Pete can't be on that homicide forever, and at least JJ said Pete hadn't had an opportunity to get it. So we know that much, and that was going to be your question to Pete, wasn't it?"

Rosie jumps in, "That's it!"

"That's it, what?"

"JJ's not going to rock the boat on his end, so we now have permission to do it on our end," proclaims Rosie exuberantly.

"What do you mean, permission?

"JJ said Pete has nothing, so my dilemma was waiting, and waiting makes me not able to think straight, and not thinking straight puts me back to rehashing. It's like a hamster in a cage with that irritating wheel going around and around."

"Really."

"Yes, but now we are free."

"Free from what?"

Rosie taps her foot and implores, "No, not free from anything. Just free to continue. I'd bet California authorities have gotten whatever they intended to, and Pete seems to be out of the picture. So let's do this!"

CONSTANCE LOUISE SINCLAIR

"You want me to do what, call Phillip? You're insane. We have no earthly idea how he is involved, and you can't even ask Pete if he has gotten any information on him."

"Okay, calm down. Maybe that idea was a little drastic," states Rosie. "So how do you feel about calling his wife? What's her name?"

Connie briefly closes one eye to signify the frustration she feels but realizes she isn't as averse to this proposition. *No, she could speak with Joyce.*

"Yes, but not in person. I'll call her."

"Great, let's do this!"

Rosie's go-get-it attitude is back and in full force. She walks to the bar where Connie has just placed her coffee to her mouth and gives her a punch to the arm.

"Oww-aa! What was that for?"

"Oh sorry, I thought you were as pumped as I am," Rosie quips.

Rosie is so excited that she has an intense desire for a big hug. Rosie, with Connie unaware, spins Connie's bar stool and hits her with a bear hug conjoined with a side-to-side rocking motion.

Connie breaks into a wide grin as Rosie often doesn't share Connie's feely-touchy need as Connie cracks, "Yeah, you're all happy-go-lucky, because you don't have to make the call."

Rosie insists, "Now you've ruined our communal moment, so call."

"I'll call, but I'm doing it my way. We shouldn't have to resort to trickery as Joyce is a friend, so we will cajole."

"Call it whatever you want, just call."

"Joyce, this is Connie. How are you?"

"Oh Constance, I have wanted to call you ever since that day at the office. Phillip was just so hurtful. I couldn't get a thing out of him, and he said we weren't going to speak about it any further, and that was that."

"Oh, you poor dear. Now I feel to blame for your situation with Phillip. I'll let you go without even asking this of you," Connie tempts.

Rosie thinks, *Whoa Connie, you are letting it spew.*

"No, Constance. I feel so ashamed. I can't imagine you could ask anything that would possibly make up for Phillip's behavior."

"No, it might make a wider gap between you two. I'll just call Phillip personally and ask him because I feel he is quite capable of getting this done speedily."

"That is just plain nonsense if I have ever heard it. Constance Sinclair, you tell me what is going on, and tell me right now, you hear?"

"It's just this dilemma arose, and believe me when I tell you it's due to my over active curiosity. But I know that Phillip frequents Becky's Circle B and probably knows everyone there, plus with his status in the community, I know Phillip would have some pull to let me see the security tapes of the day the cell phones were purchased."

Connie stops. She stands deathly still with hand over her mouth and unwavering eye contact with Rosie. Connie fans herself with folded napkins from the counter, because she is absolutely out of breath from her non-stop disclosure. She knows if she stopped, the conversation might change to a different subject, and she doesn't want to have to wrangle it back in the direction of her choosing.

After an extended time, Connie is sure Joyce knows of no way around calling Phillip, Connie adds, "I certainly understand, Joyce, and forgive me for asking you to help with my problem. Joyce, are you there?"

"Yes, I am. I was just going through my sorority club's yearbook. I can't think of her name, but one of her daughters, Constance, she is the sweetest little thing. Well you won't believe this. She works at Becky's, and I gave Charlotte, that's her name, Charlotte, well I gave Charlotte the most darlin' formal evening wear, and she was just so appreciative and said her daughter had just the place to wear it. Constance, it was the one with the pink iridescent ruffles to the waist, and I'm sure you remember the ruffles extended to the sleeves. I had told her I would get the matching shoes and purse to her before the big event, and now I'm gonna throw in the tiara as well, that is if she comes to our rescue. I'm sure she will speak to her daughter!"

"Joyce, that is wonderful, and aren't you the most generous person on this earth to help that poor sweet thing like that, but I'm really under a time crunch, so I bet Phillip could expedite the matter more quickly as he is so well known in the community."

"Poppy cock! He is no better known than I, and if that child is working, I'll have a copy in no time, especially if it coincides with her boss Dennis' lunch hour. I'll call Penny, Dennis' wife, right now and see when Dennis takes his lunch. You know, Constance. Penny is in sorority!"

ROSIE REDMOND ROSEMAN

"Come on, get in the car," prompts Rosie.

"Where to?"

"Enid. Let's head up to the Chapman's and be at least accessible when Joyce calls with the tape."

Connie counters, "I didn't tell her to call my cell."

"I'm certain if she can't contact you at home, she will try your cell. And besides, I want that tape in our hands before her husband gets home, and she has a chance to reveal our intentions, as he might just have a different idea in the matter."

"Oh, I didn't think of that," states Connie.

"I'd also like to visit Becky's," Rosie states as she tries to locate the clock for the time as Connie starts the car.

"Why do you want to go to Becky's?

"Just for green," replies Rosie as she stares out the window.

"Just for green? What the heck does that mean?"

"You know. It's kinda like, just because I can. Where's the clock???"

"The clock is right there under the navigation system. See! I think we have been through this before."

Rosie gives a slow grrrr of agitation as she questions, "What kind of car is this? It looks like it has diamond head and tail lights but doesn't have a decent clock. That clock doesn't even have numerals. Still, think you got gypped."

"You're just on edge. You're not good at cooling your jets."

Rosie glances at Connie and asks, "Cooling my what?"

Connie laughs and adds, "Just getting even with you for your 'just for green' comment.

Okay, Miss Car Dissector, it's 3:05. Now, what does that tell you?"

"Well, it's still early enough to get the tape from Joyce and also hit Becky's before heading back from Enid."

"What do you think we can find at Becky's?"

"I haven't a clue. Something in my head just tells me to go. Sometimes I don't even know what I expect to find until I'm in that moment."

"That's good enough for me," replies Connie as she remembers Rosie's identical train-of-thought upon entering Ludlow's office before they were carted off to jail. Connie starts to bemoan that previous situation as the ending to that adventure was jail, maybe not a perfect option at this time, but just then her phone rings.

"Hello, Joyce."

"Hi, Constance. I tried your house, and there was no answer."

"I'm in the car."

"I was expecting Consuela to answer. Is Consuela not with you any longer?"

"No, not daily, she just comes every other week."

"Oh, I see. But Phillip had given me the impression that the estate was back to normal since the prototype was in production and…"

Rosie perks at Joyce's hesitance, bends forward and rolls her hand in a manner to relate to Connie to prod for more information.

"And what, Joyce?"

"Oh, nothing, I hesitated, because I just overheard Phillip on the phone, and I can't remember his exact words but something to do with an additional disclosure of some type. Anyway, Dennis is at a Lion's meeting at Golden Corral so that problem is solved."

"What time are you to pick up the tape?"

"That's why I'm calling. I don't have to pick the tape up as Charlotte said Stacey, her daughter, told her she could just email it. She knew what I was talking about as some agency in California had requested the same tape. I'm to call Stacey with my email address, but I'm going just to give her yours. Is it still the same, Constancesinclair@live.com?"

CONSTANCE LOUISE SINCLAIR

"That was a short drive to the entrance gate and back," denotes Connie.

Rosie heads up the stairs while Connie continues to the kitchen.

"Where are you going?" asks Rosie.

"To grab something to eat."

"We just ate."

"Well, I don't feel like it. I think I was too mad even to remember lunch, and all of this makes me want to munch. Go ahead and turn on the laptop. I'll be right up. Passwords are under the desk calendar."

Rosie answers, "Pink sticky note on right-hand side?"

"Yup, you got it."

Rosie opens the laptop and reaches under the calendar and retrieves the note, still torn in half exactly as Ludlow had left it, and just then, she feels chills on her arms."

Rosie looks up and says, "Hello Charles. We're getting there as fast as we can. You know, you could be a little more help, ole buddy, don't you?" Rosie leans back and runs her hands over her arms in overwhelming astonishment and wonder.

DOUGLAS HARTLY

"Amanda, follow me. I want you to see them."

"The babies? Oh, yes. Look at them! They are so lively."

Doug cautions, "But only two mommas are settled enough to accept a greeting from us. I'll grab a bucket of oats, and that will bring them closer. You grab a lead."

"What's the count now?" queries Amanda as she follows closely behind Doug.

"Five in all. Three colts and two fillies."

"Doesn't matter. Boys or girls, I love them all."

"See," states Doug. "These two mares are broke to the bucket. I need to tell Jose and the others what a good job they have done."

Amanda slowly, but cautiously, approaches the mare and snaps a lead in place on her halter and turns to the beautiful black colt softly smelling Amanda's outreached hand.

"He could be Magic's son. Just look at him."

The colt shows no fear as he suckles Amanda's fingers.

"Come here, you beautiful black beauty," implores Amanda as he readily accepts the tender scratches to his ears and neck.

"He's mine. I'm claiming him right now. Please let him be mine! Come here, my Black Beauty!"

Doug chuckles, encircles Amanda with his arms, not only physically but, at that moment, he emotionally knows in his heart, that he can never live one day without her.

ROSIE REDMOND ROSEMAN

"Man. Let me back that up. Oh no."

"What?" asks Connie.

"The tape starts with him at the counter," decries Rosie.

"So?"

"I need to see him full view walking into the store. I want to see his demeanor and actions before he gets to the counter. Especially his gait."

"Well, go ahead and start. I want to see his face and see if he was seated behind me at the airport. Please Lord, help us get this figured out."

Rosie stands and adds, "You sit, and I'll stand."

Connie pulls the chair in position and taps the play icon. The tape shows him at the counter head down as he pays cash for the phones.

"Come on, look up," insists Connie.

As if at Connie's urging, he looks toward the back and asks something as he adjusts his cap down. The clerk reaches for the item he mentions and places cigarettes on the counter. Just as she grasps the cash, he places his hand down to stop her, shakes his head and taps the cigarettes away and replaces them with a package of gum.

Rosie informs, "Reformed smoker about to relapse."

"I think that's him. If he hadn't adjusted that cap," Connie states.

"Close enough," implies Rosie.

Connie continues, "There was a glimpse of his eyes. Did you see his emotionless eyes? Unyielding. All just the same as at LAX."

"Well, I can't be positive, but I think that is the man at Driscoll's. But that is only a snippet of the footage I was hoping for," bemoans Rosie. "I need movement. I want to see him exiting the store, and we would know his height and can compare to the video of him as he enters your bedroom door."

"Thanks for bringing that back to mind. You know, I never watched that with you and Pete for a reason. I didn't want that image in my mind."

"Oh, sorry, honey."

"That's okay. Where's my phone? I'm texting JJ to check his email. Don't you think they need to see this?"

"Yes, the more heads, the better," states Rosie.

Connie rubs the back of her neck as she hits send on the security video and asks, "Did you notice which door he was exiting at Founders, because I saw absolutely nothing."

"Yup, you were giving me the scenic guided tour of the Oklahoma City skyline."

"But no door?" queries Connie.

"No, do you know whose offices are in that area?" asks Rosie.

"Not really. I usually enter and leave at the front reception area. But, you know what, Rosie? We can rule out Deidra Hulbert."

"We sure can. She was gone long before we saw this guy and…"

"And what?" queries Connie.

"When's your next appointment at the attorneys?" ask Rosie as a gleam enters her eyes.

"Day after tomorrow. And what?"

"We might be able to use that little kernel of knowledge while we're there, but now, look at these coins."

"What am I looking for? They look identical."

Rosie instructs, "Close your eyes."

"What is it with you that you always want me defenseless with my eyes closed?" Aggressively states Connie.

"It just seems like you can't switch senses, so you need to close your eyes to access all your abilities. Give me the coins, and sit here."

Connie mocks, "Connie, sit here. Close your eyes." Connie thinks. *You sure are bossy.*

"I'm having you sit down, so I don't have to pick you up off the floor. Now hold your hands out."

Rosie places one coin in each hand, and asks, "Do you feel the difference?"

Connie opens her eyes and answers, "Yes. This one is heavier."

"Good," continues Rosie. "Close your eyes, and rub both of them at the same time."

"Oh, Rosie, the heavier one has a slight protrusion."

"Exactly," adds Rosie. "I was so focused on the coin when the keys came in the mail, I was convinced Charles wanted us to figure out the coin, but no. The keys were for the titles and for us to find the fourth coin.

"So we know the coin is important, because Pete told us that certain coins had different levels of accessibility," Connie states with great eagerness and a positive outlook.

Rosie says, "So you know what I'm thinking?"

"Yup."

"You got keys to get us in if one of these on Charles' keys don't work?"

"Better than that. I know where Charles' access card is. We just tap it," declares Connie.

"Great. Get up. Let's go."

SINCLAIR OIL COMPANY

"How much longer do we have to wait?" asked Connie.

"At least thirty minutes from whenever we see anybody leave. I've seen two more lights go off so make yourself comfortable. Then we have to time our entry after the outside security truck passes."

Connie admits, "I think I'm overcoming some of my fear. I won't be sticking so close to you anymore."

"Well, that's good. Feeling a little liberated, are we?"

"I don't know about liberated. Maybe I'm losing a few inhibitions, and I know I am feeling more optimistic. I think we have this figured out."

Rosie sharing Connie's eagerness replies, "Still several things on the list that need answers."

"Like what? You have ruled out the Wilsons. Ruled out Deidra. We know Phillip is hiding something, but you said it was of no importance, right?"

Rosie turns in her seat and confesses, "Yup, but I still haven't ticked off the list that little piece of information Joyce alluded to about Phillip implying something about an additional disclosure of some type. I'm certain that has to fit in here someplace."

Rosie reaches for her door handle and decrees, "There goes security. Let's do this."

Entry is a breeze. Rosie pulls Connie behind her as they both flatten against the wall. Rosie points to the security camera as they both inch toward the stairwell door.

Safely inside, Rosie asks, "What floor is Charles' office?"

"Three."

"This will be a workout."

Rosie fiddles with the keys and gains entry on the second try. The lights flick on, tempering both girls' positive outlook, as they remember entry into Louis Ludlow's office at the Oil Tower. They follow the same protocol as then by securing the blinds.

Rosie looks to Connie and asks, "What's wrong? You okay?"

"I'm good, but when the lights came on, I thought, please don't let this end with us sitting in jail as it did at the Oil Tower."

"Not a chance," says Rosie as she retrieves the coin from her pocket, "because you are the boss's wife, this time." Rosie places the coin on the middle drawer of Charles' desk and continues down both sides. She twirls the chair towards the credenza and begins with the drawers on the left. She finishes the middle set of drawers and turns toward the last set, but Connie is standing in her way.

Rosie looks up, and Connie is displaying a framed photo. Rosie leans back and lets out a slow whistle as she sees Phillip with Deidra Hulbert arm in arm on the golf course.

Connie concludes, “I guess we know a little nugget about Phillip. All I need to find now is a photo of Charles and Margaret. All men are the same.”

The moment the words leave her lips, she regrets them. “Rosie, certainly not Pete. Never Pete.”

Rosie exhales, “It’s okay. Let me do these drawers.”

Connie lays the picture aside and watches as nothing yields to the touch of the coin. Rosie rises, heads to the far end of the room to the conference table and seating area. “Help me turn these chairs.”

They continue with the couch and leave it tilted due to the weight. Still nothing. Both try to grab a breath as Connie has her hands on her hips, and Rosie is slightly tilted with her hands on her knees. “No floor safe.”

Connie and Rosie lean back against the overturned sofa and stare mindlessly towards Charles desk. Simultaneously, they both head for the large picture hanging between the two bookcases on each side of the credenza. Connie tries the right side, but it doesn’t budge as Rosie tries the left and nothing. In disgust, Connie hits the corner of the frame and as if in answer, it begins to raise slowly revealing the safe.

Connie is first to speak. “How does it open? There is no visible locking mechanism?”

Rosie takes the coin and starts methodically on the edge of the safe. No reaction on either side or bottom. She can’t reach the top, but Connie quickly clears the area, and Rosie crawls on the credenza. She begins, and the moment the coin crosses the middle, they hear the click.

Rosie jumps down as their discovery is massive. Cash, bearer bonds and yes, deeds. The moment she lifts the deeds, she feels Charles' presence and she looks up and says, "Thank you, baby."

Rosie says, "What can we put all this in? And let's get out of here?"

Connie moves toward the trash can as they hear movement at the door.

Rosie slams the safe, and the picture starts its slow journey back in place.

"Come on! Close, close."

LOS ANGELES COUNTY SHERIFF'S DEPARTMENT

JJ stares into the large mirror facing the stainless steel table he sits behind. He wonders if his decision to come without an attorney was wise. *I have nothing to hide, right? Isn't that what Dwayne said? Just drop by for a quick conversation about the incident at the ranch.*

But he knows better than that. He has been deceived and lured, and yet here he sits. *I will use the same strategy as I did in Oklahoma. What could they possibly know that I don't? There will be no reason to show surprise! Remain confident in all my answers, and stay composed.*

"Hello, Mr. Paige. Do you mind if we record this interview?"

JJ nods approval as he waits to see if he is read his rights under the Miranda Warning. If so, this interview will quickly turn into an interrogation.

He tries to contain his insecurities as he holds on to the small feeling of comfort that comes when the conversation continues.

"For the record, I am Undersheriff Lynn Morris, and this is Deputy Dwayne Johnson. You are Jeremiah Jason Paige, is that correct?"

"Yes."

"As you know, I had questioned the registration of a trailer at your location and Douglas Hartly claimed ownership through an LLC Corporation. Do you remember that?"

"Yes."

"I asked that question as the burner phones used in connection with the home invasion were purchased in Oklahoma. You can see where that might raise some flags don't you, Mr. Paige?"

"Yes."

"Well, with those flags, I felt that checking you and Mr. Hartly through NCIC was warranted. Mr. Hartly had no record, wants or warrants but not you, Mr. Paige. Do you know what we found?"

JJ is slow to answer, hoping that this is a rhetorical question, but after a short pause, he answers, "Yes, I was held as a Material Witness in a murder case."

JJ offers nothing further, as he doesn't want to open any avenue to allow continuance of questions.

"That's all you have to offer?"

"Yes, unless your information didn't reveal I was released with no further action taken."

"No, that was the outcome of our inquiry."

The Undersheriff rises and walks to the mirrored area and asks, "Also, when we visited you at your ranch, let's see, is it your ranch or Mr. Hartly's ranch?"

JJ thinks, *where would they even get the idea the ranch is Doug's? What could...*

"Mr. Paige, who is Jessie Sinclair?" Then as the Undersheriff turns, and with a furrow to his brow, says, "An even better question, where is Jessie Sinclair?"

OKLAHOMA CITY POLICE DEPARTMENT INTERROGATION ROOM

"When are you going to tell them? Just ask for him. It did me no good to tell them who I am," bemoans Connie.

"I think the kicker on that was when they asked for identification, they noticed that people breaking and entering don't carry purses." Rosie adds.

Connie declares, "I showed the security guard Charles entry card, but I wasn't feeling that secure with his abilities, the way he was waving that gun around. Is that legal?"

"I think that's the least of our problems now, and the funny thing is…"

"Funny?" Connie quips.

"Yes, let me finish. The funny thing is if you have to contact an attorney, who are you going to call?" Rosie smirks big time.

Connie states, "You're right. Oh, my. Rosie, we got the safe covered, but where is the coin? Driscolls can't get the coin."

Rosie leans in close and whispers, "In my bra, so we can't be arrested, because a strip search wouldn't go well."

Connie exclaims, "Heaven forbid. Strip search?"

The door opens, and a familiar voice full of déjà vu mocks, "Hello, ladies, would you please follow me to booking?"

Rosie fusses, "Danny, that's not funny. Where's Pete?"

Danny in a full belly laugh shuts the door and answers, "He's on his way. I tried to wait, but traffic has him held up, but I didn't want him to miss this. He went ballistic when he heard the unit go 10-8 enroute to station with Constance Sinclair and Rosie Redmond."

"How much trouble are we in?" Connie asks while shaking her head.

Danny decrees, "You do realize that one of these days it won't matter who you are or who you are married to. There are things that are beyond anyone's control and especially pay grade."

Rosie states, "I know. I'm so sorry. Is Pete in trouble? He can't lose his job, or even worse, get busted to a lower grade."

"Well, for now, Rosie Redmond is at the station and not Rosie Roseman. When he called me, he was not happy. Maybe traffic will give him time to decompress a little."

"So, Danny, what happens next? It was all my fault, Rosie was just an innocent bystander."

"Yup, right. Like anyone that knows you two would believe that. Wait here."

Danny leaves, and Rosie growls, "Really. Wait here? We're in a locked interrogation room."

Connie asks, "Aren't you the least bit scared?"

Rose, with a dreamy smile, answers, "You remember the last time we were in jail, and you were all jack-jawed over JJ, and you knew he was gonna come for us, and I said how envious I was of you to have found love a second time?"

"Awe, yeah, I remember. You said I would have to be a bird and fly out the jail cell windows."

"Well, guess what?"

"What?"

"I'm not envious any longer. Even if Pete is hoppin' mad, I know he loves me with a forever and always love."

As the door opens, their laughter is interrupted. Pete enters.

SINCLAIR ESTATE

"That was a slight embarrassment," admits Connie.

"It worked, and we're home."

"Yes, thank you. Lord," Connie prays, "But to be identified as Constance Sinclair by my old booking photo. Really! And thank you, Lord, that you were never recognized as Roseman."

"Oh, I think that little farce won't last long. I'm certain there will be repercussions."

"We need to get some sleep."

"Sleep?" exclaims Rosie.

"We're not going to bed until we figure out what to do, how to get the safe contents legally. I wonder if anyone else knows of the safe, and if so, about the contents. And what about the contents? Bearer bonds, cash! Sweetheart, forgive me but no reflection on Charles, could this be ill gotten gains?"

"Rosie that mind of yours, always full of questions. One thing's for sure, you're right. I have no legal representation, and if we remove all that, can I just deposit it in my account or…"

"Exactly, or…?"

JEREMIAH JASON PAIGE

JJ paces the length of the sables his mind running rampant. Where had he gotten the idea that Amanda has title to the ranch? After all, it has been called Bordillon Ranch from the moment Margaret moved here shortly after Amanda was born. Margaret had kept Bordillon as her last name after her divorce, but she had been divorced years before Amanda was born.

It was Margaret. Yes, she had said Charles was transferring funds to a trust that would stabilize the ranch and continue support for Amanda.

CONSTANCE LOUISE SINCLAIR

"I'm wondering if I need to keep the appointment with Arthur, even after we think the weird guy is associated somehow with them."

"You've already told Arthur it is about a title to property. You need to find a new attorney, so we can get stuff from Charles' safe, but to just quit Driscoll's all at once will be a red flag for certain. If you ever are going to feel safe, someone needs to be exposed."

"Need I remind you, Mrs. Roseman, the admonishing we both took at the police department?"

FOUNDER'S TOWER

"Okay, get over here, and I'll be back as quickly as possible."

Connie turns in her seat as she places the car in park and declares, "Are you serious?"

"Why do you find that so shocking?" counters Rosie.

"I don't know. I just assumed that everyone knew how."

"Nope, never did. I took driver's ed but had a bad experience, so I just take the bus when needed."

"Glad we haven't been in a pinch where I expected you to drive. Besides, when I said it might look strange you going in with me to see Arthur on personal business, you said you'd just wait. I thought you meant take the car and drop me off."

"No, I meant I'll wait at reception, or I'll start waiting at reception."

Connie chides, "Hang on to the car keys so you can wait in the car, because I'm not planning on lingering. Rosie, what do you have up your sleeve?"

Rosie chuckles and adds, "For me to know and for you to find out. Now see, I understand that lingo."

PETER ROSEMAN

"No, the girls are okay, but that was a close call for all concerned. But they know not to go off on their own again. We have to keep in better contact. I figured Rosie would be distraught about the late nights. You know, I told you she was back to full mind mode."

Danny admits, "Yup, this isn't much of a life for you staying at the apartment and Rosie still at the estate."

"You can say that again, Pete adds as his voice trails off and then, "Danny!"

"What?"

"Rosie isn't at all upset about me staying at the apartment. Do you think she should be?"

"No, she just respects your profession and understands, that's all. Rosie's not like Cheryl," Danny continues, "This job is why both of my marriages imploded. Broken dinner dates and missed parties. Cheryl always said with a smile, 'I'll just find widows row and blend right in.'"

"Oh Danny, everyone deserves someone to grow old with."

"It's okay, good comes from all things. I've got the girls, and they still love me."

"That's true. Let's see, Susie, Beth, and what's the baby's name?"

Danny with a smile shakes his head and answers, "Celsie. Celsie's the baby. You all planning on a family?"

Pete rises as the jovial mood is replaced with feelings of circumstances that may be beyond his ability to control. "Danny, there is something I haven't told Rosie."

"About children?"

"Yes, the time has never seemed right."

DRISCOLL LAW FIRM

Before the doors even close and the elevator begins to ascend, Connie nervously asks, "What are you up to? I just want to make the appointment and leave."

"Nothing. I might have to meander down the hall and take a bathroom break or two."

The doors open, and Rosie chimes, "Drats, the restrooms are right here? That's not very luxurious."

"Good, that will keep you out of trouble.

Hello, I'm Constance Sinclair, and I have an appointment with Arthur."

"Yes, I know, Mrs. Sinclair. Good to see you again. I'll let CJ know you all are here."

"Oh, I'll be seeing Arthur and my friend will wait if you don't mind."

"Yes," Rosie cajoles. "I'll be waiting." Then in a lower tone, "and waiting…"

"If you're not a magazine peruser, we have several beautiful aquariums."

"That's great. How many are there?"

"Several all along the outer corridor to the south and around."

Rosie quickly acclaims, "Perfect!" Which makes Connie involuntarily flinch.

ARTHUR DRISCOLL

"Mrs. Sinclair, do come in. Please be seated. Is there anything CJ could get for you? Coffee, tea, a beverage?"

"Coffee would be perfect. Black, please."

"How have things been going since last we met? I know it was a difficult time for you and not an easy situation in which you found yourself."

"How very true. I had a lot to learn, and the learning curve was intense, but that seems to be behind me."

"That's good. You have some questions on property. Is this about a purchase and verification of obtaining a clean title? If so, let me see if Matthew is available as he handles probate and title litigation."

"I'm not certain," Connie states as she struggles to hand the two Abstracts of Title to him."

"Let me help you, that's quite a bundle," Arthur states as he takes the cumbersome documents and continues with, "Let's sit at the conference table where we have a clean area to better view these."

Connie gathers her purse and coffee and joins him as he holds her chair for her to be seated. Tinges of realization that she misses a gentleman's attention return.

"Awe," Arthur states. "I never tire of seeing brief glimpses of Oklahoma history and holding documents signed by the President of the United States at a distinct time in history. This is an Abstract of Title to lands never owned before, and further it is title No. 6. These lands, during this time, were not true titles but under Character of Instrument listed 'Patent' and dated July 3, 1897. And most interesting, for Grantees Consideration, which acknowledges the amount paid, it just shows $ Premises. This is truly the beginning of the beginning."

He continues, "The United States of America, by the President, William McKinley, Grantors to I.M. Waller, Grantees. Is this a relative of Charles'?"

"No, actually, Irena Mae was my great, great grandmother. She made the run when she was in her early 30's with her two young sons. Her husband, Abner, stayed in Iowa and worked the rails and sent money until she got established. I always thought it interesting that she maintained all the lands only in her name. There was possibly some advantage to the family to keep it that way. Upon her death, Abner received a child's portion of her estate."

"Yes, I believe that might be true, also, as I have seen other documents listing females as sole ownership. There were several ways of obtaining land: one was by the runs, five total; two were by land lotteries, and then there was even one by sealed bid."

Connie sees the time moving past and thinks she doesn't want to pay for an Oklahoma history lesson as she states, "My endeavor today is to ascertain why these documents weren't included during the time of our meeting to verify assets?"

"Yes, I can see where you might question that, but during that meeting, we were attempting to value all personal assets so as to avoid the sale of real property. I'm sure you will agree that our efforts were rewarded."

Connie's due diligence waivers briefly as she admits, "I do agree and thank God I was able to keep my home."

"I know you do, and I'm glad Driscoll and Driscoll could help with that."

Connie, after a brief exhale of emotion, asks, "What about the second document. Could you shed some light on that?"

Arthur scans the top couple of pages and then flips to the back section. He retrieves a legal pad from his desk and notates items.

Connie hears her phone vibrate in her purse but ignores it choosing to let it go to voicemail.

Arthur returns his attention to Connie, but only briefly as he states, "Please excuse me a moment as I need to get verification on something."

Connie smiles and answers, "Certainly." She hears her phone a second time. Her hand is in her purse before Arthur has completely exited through the side doorway.

Connie sees it is Rosie and feels the urgency as she knows she wouldn't be calling once, much less twice, unless it is important.

Connie answers quickly with, "What?"

Rosie rapidly starts with, "I'll make this quick. Just a heads-up to watch yourself as I found out that weird guy was employed as an investigator same as Hulbert but more precisely used as a bodyguard."

Connie straightens and exclaims, "Bodyguard for…" but without even a goodbye, Rosie terminates the call.

Connie absorbs the word, "bodyguard" and thinks, *who is being threatened to the point of needing protection,* while she returns her phone to her purse as it vibrates indicating a voicemail.

She curls and uncurls her fingers around the phone as she waits for recent calls to appear. She is at the point of frustration over Rosie's discovery, but ever so quickly that emotion is replaced with disbelief and peppered with fear as the name of the missed call is illuminated the same moment Arthur re-enters the room.

PHILLIP CHAPMAN

Phillip leans back in his chair and exhales as he waits for Matthew to accept his call. Connie is obviously not going to answer, but Matthew keeps urging me to find out what the bank turned up.

Phillip's mind returns to the golf course where he, Matthew, Arthur, and Charles were enjoying a leisurely foursome. Who would have thought answering Matthew's query by repeating Charles phone conversation could be so unfortunate for Phillip. I know it has to do with a deed. No, it was deeds. Yes, Charles had said, "Need to get keys back. That's the only way to get to the deeds. I need to tell Connie about this as the keys are the only way to access the deeds."

"Mr. Chapman?"

"Yes!"

"Mr. Driscoll is unavailable. Would you like me to transfer you to his voicemail?"

"Yes, please." Phillip impatiently waits for Matthews's taped introduction to cease and, in his haste to spew his contempt, has to start over as he hears the beep seconds into his message. "Dang it, this is it Matt. I'm done, you keep pushing, and I'm telling Joyce about Deidra. You'll have nothing to use as leverage."

"Hello, Phillip. Glad I could catch your call. I want you to know, the firm does not need a second investigator, and his employee has been terminated."

"Oh Matt, that is wonderful. When?"

"That's what I was doing when your call came in. I had concluded that possibly nefarious things might have happened, and the danger not only to my livelihood as an attorney but the reputation of this firm was being compromised. He's cleaning out his desk as we speak."

ARTHUR DRISCOLL

"Sorry to keep you waiting, but had to confer on this last document."

Connie's anticipation heightens over the California certificate as she awaits further disclosure from Arthur. Why would he feel it necessary to consult on this? Could this be the Bordillon ranch? She feels her palms moisten while she adjusts her chair squarely to the conference table, and Arthur is seated.

"Mrs. Sinclair, I'm not certain of the degree of your knowledge with abstracts, so I don't know how much you want to know, or better to ask, desire to know?"

Connie finds herself, once again, under control of her emotions with a momentary lowering of her eyes. She smiles and nods as she answers, "No, please enlighten me. As I said earlier, the learning curve into the business aspects of my life seems to be presenting itself again and again. I like to think I have become resilient. No, I know I'm now well-seasoned. Strong to the point that I can function better under pressure as it seems I have to succeed with it more and more. Please continue."

Arthur lifts the Oklahoma property abstract and places it in the middle of the table and continues, "In Oklahoma, an abstract company is used to verify the accuracy of the title to real property. Their certification assures they have researched as far back as necessary, which is usually back to the last sale date. They search records at the courthouse for any activity such as liens to verify that there are no problems or as we say, no clouds found in the title and when they issue an abstract of title, they certify and guarantee that that is true and correct."

Connie nods acknowledgment of her understanding.

Arthur picks up the remaining document and continues, "California doesn't recognize abstract companies as the influx of miners during the gold rush days preceded any semblance of legal organization. California's statehood was still well into the future."

Arthur leans back in his chair as he chuckles, "That being said, the aforementioned 'semblance of legality' was not entirely accurate as there were attorneys-at-law present and as such, they offered their services or should I admit, provided their legal expertise in the robust debate of ownership. With no abstract companies to guarantee title, California issues a Certification of Title with an attorney's opinion attached. The opinion is an attorney's guarantee of a person's land ownership. Now, we need to look towards the back of this document and see if an attorney's guarantee is present and, yes, it is. So what we have here is a California Certificate of Title to ownership of California real property."

Connie leans forward and with a furrowed brow asks, "Is there a physical address attached in the document or just the legal description?"

Arthur directs, "Let's begin here. Who is Jessie Sinclair?"

"Well, I can't be certain, but I'm assuming Charles' great grandparent or possibly great-great grandparent. And with Jessie for a first name, I'm not even certain of gender."

"Is there any further paperwork that you possibly have?"

"Such as?"

"I'm looking for paperwork that will bridge the gap in time between Jessie Sinclair to Charles."

"I can look," states Connie. "This would be additional legal documents like a will?"

"Well yes, but it also could be quit claim deeds that would have been utilized to transfer ownership expeditiously."

"Mr. Driscoll, I was hoping for more information on your part and…"

"I understand, Mrs. Sinclair, but we will have to look into several aspects of ownership before I can definitively give you any further answers. Anything I offer now is purely speculation in reference to the California title, but I will start the process of getting the Oklahoma property moved solely into your name. With your approval, I'll retain these papers and get back to you at a later date," he states while they both rise.

Connie walks behind him as he opens the office door and Arthur states, "I'll have CJ show you out."

Connie looks at CJ and smiles acceptance but then sees Rosie seated in the waiting area and abruptly halts forcing Arthur Driscoll to pull back or be forced to bump Connie forward.

Rosie's presence jars Connie to the realization of Rosie's disclosure that the intruder is employed at the firm and more than likely in the close vicinity at this very moment.

Connie turns, which places her in close juxtaposition with Arthur and while maintaining firm eye contact with him, affirms with a stoic face and matter-of-fact attitude. "CJ, please make copies of my documents for Arthur as I have decided to keep the originals in my possession."

CONSTANCE LOUISE SINCLAIR

"Okay, we're safely in the elevator. Are you certain of your information?"

Rosie affirms, "Well, let's just say my self-guided tour through the aquatic world ended in a chance meeting with one of the secretaries."

"Really," answers Connie.

Rosie leans in to continue her disclosure as the elevator doors open and they exit at the Lobby level. "I intended to meander in the hopes of a face-to-face encounter with Kirby."

"Who?"

"Oh sorry, I'm getting ahead of myself." Rosie clears her throat and points, "Give the guy your ticket, and let's get the car."

Connie complies, and the valet jogs out of sight.

Rosie continues, "Yup, weird guy's name is Kirby. She was talking pretty fast, and I was speed walking to keep up with her, so didn't catch anything else."

"So you just stop someone in the hall and said, 'Can you tell me who weird guy is?'" Connie continues in disbelief.

"Not exactly. I just happened to be by one of the restrooms. Here's the car. Get in, and let's stop for lunch. Your pick and I can finish.

"No way," Connie challenges adamantly.

"You're kidding, right. Last time we left here, you were upset with me, because you wanted lunch, and here I'm trying to make up for not stopping, and besides I'm starved."

"We're getting home. I want to look over the California papers and, oh my…"

"Oh, my." Connie, oh my, what?"

Connie is rapidly navigating her car menu before driving away, until she reaches voicemail and selects the read option. The female narrator begins, "Would you like me to play your last voice mail?" Connie answers, "Yes, please."

Rosie leans forward in anticipation of the message just as she sees who she believes to be Kirby pull onto NW Highway in a black sedan. "Go, Connie, go. Go now!" Rosie exclaims in an almost scream. "Turn right, speed up!" All calamity breaks loose as Phillip Chapman drones on in the background during the melee.

"Connie, this is Phillip. You clearly aren't returning my calls so I feel compelled to leave this message. You need to know, I'd been coerced to gain information from you regarding bank files. All of this originated from a call I innocently overheard where Charles was speaking of deeds. That is what they want. It has to be deeds. Please forgive me. I hope this is helpful."

JEREMIAH JASON PAIGE

"Connie, I got your message, and we all have…"

Rosie instructs, "Connie, speed up. It's a black sedan, and it's a couple of blocks ahead."

"Connie, are you there? What's going on?" JJ excitedly questions.

"Go, Connie, go. Change lanes. Don't get too close. Okay, to the right."

"Connie, are you…"

"JJ, I can't talk."

ROSIE REDMOND ROSEMAN

"That's him. I feel it in my bones. Where are we anyhow? I'm lost, we've made too many turns."

Connie takes a few quick breaths and sighs, "I'm glad we're out of that noon hour traffic and all the maneuvering I was doing, I'm surprised I kept up."

Rosie asks, "I know we're south of NW Highway, but then, where?"

"We just turned off of Piedmont Road. See this is the Clydesdales Barn on our right."

Rosie perplexed, "Clydesdales?"

"Rosie, you have to have heard of the Express Clydesdales Ranch. They are world famous! There he is. Looks like he's taking Foreman towards the west. This is the back way into El Reno."

"Really, couldn't prove it by me," Rosie states while she shakes her head.

"He must be headed to El Reno, but why didn't he just take the Kilpatrick and stay on the good road?"

"Where'd he go?" Connie blurts. "I just looked down at my speedometer, and now I've lost him."

Rosie rolls her window down and directs, "I think he went north. What's out here anyway?"

"The river, mostly."

"Slow down. You see it?"

"No, what?"

"That dust trail. Slow down!"

"Okay, okay, I'm slowing."

Rosie points, "There's a sign."

"Where?"

"On that barbed wire. Let me out. Stop!"

Connie stops just after passing the road.

Rosie bolts from the car, wades through the Johnson grass-filled ditch to the fence where she rubs the rusted sign. She glances Connie's way as she pulls her phone from her pocket and snaps a picture before returning to the car. Connie shakes her head in disbelief as Rosie has tickle grass in her hair and stick-tights attached to her clothes.

"Why did you take a picture? After you moved the weeds, I could read it from here. Private Property of Oklahoma Gun Club."

"You think," cautions Rosie as she brings the photo into view. "Is that what it says?"

Connie places the car in park, leans over the console, squints as she asks, "What are those black spots?"

"Gunshot holes!" As they make wide-eyed eye contact, Rosie announces, "Let me read this to you. It reads, 'Private Property of OK Gun Club' and not 'Oklahoma Gun Club' as you surmised."

Rosie locates her bag in the back floor board and frantically digs as she shifts her purse from side to side.

"What do you need?" questions Connie.

"I need to find the keys. Charles' keys."

"You have them with you?"

"Well, yes," Rosie answers matter-of-factly. "I want to see the second key. You know, the one marked with the initials 'OK'."

"You think this is the location the key opens?"

"Only one way to find out!"

CONSTANCE LOUISE SINCLAIR

"Rosie, please quit pacing."

"It helps me think, besides I'm mad. Can't believe how naïve I am. I thought I was being observant.

"How's your ankle?"

"It's okay. It will be fine."

"I'm so sorry," notes Rosie.

"It's not your fault," declares Connie. "I should have been the lookout instead of being stuck to you like glue. I'm such a scaredy-cat. Oh, Rosie, I try to be brave and bold like you but…"

"Honey, it's all right. We just need to figure out where we are."

"Where we are is locked in a dark dungeon."

"No, where are we, location wise. My cell phone's dead, and you left yours in the car along with your purse."

"I didn't want to be encumbered if I had to run, but I think I know what this is," Connie offers. "But I didn't know it still existed."

"Okay, you have my full attention. Go on."

"Years ago the Department of Wildlife, specifically, the game rangers for Canadian County, used a trapper who took excess wildlife, turkeys, deer, pheasant, etc. and released them at a location to repopulate the area. I think it even had a gun range built into the bank of the North Canadian River where members came to shoot and hunt."

"So you're telling me this is it, the hunting and gun club? Then where is everyone?"

"The cabins I saw looked vacant or even if anyone still comes here, it's probably on the weekends."

Rosie's pacing stops as she bemoans, "Oh my!"

Connie becomes completely still. "What is it, Rosie?"

Rosie laments, "It's only Thursday."

JEREMIAH JASON PAIGE

"Pete, this is JJ."

"Hey, JJ. Let me call you back."

"No, Pete, listen to me. Have you talked to the girls?"

"Yes, I spoke with Rosie last night and…"

"No, have you talked to them today? Specifically around lunch time?"

"JJ, what's happened? What's going on?"

CONSTANCE LOUISE SINCLAIR

"Rosie, you got any other ideas? We've tried every nook and cranny. You'd think there would be at least one window somewhere."

"Nope, we're out of options and the only crack I see tells me it's getting dark. Let's just think positive. Pete always calls before he goes to bed. We never miss talking every night even if we aren't together. The only problem with that is it could be anytime between now and midnight. Never know, just depends on when he gets out of the station."

Rosie, continues, "Surely, they ought to be getting close to wrapping that murder case up. Come on, Pete, call. Figure this out, unless, unless, he might have already called.

Connie, where are you? Am I just talking to myself? What are you doing??"

Connie, in a subdued voice whispers, "I'm praying!"

PETER ROSEMAN

"Still no answer on Connie's phone, and Rosie's goes right to voice mail."

"Try your app locator for Rosie's phone again," offers Danny.

"The app won't work if her phone's not on. We're almost to the estate to see if they are in the car or the truck and then we can put an APB out on the vehicle. JJ was adamant that they were in the car, but we need to be sure. He thinks they were in pursuit of someone in a black sedan."

"In pursuit from where? We have to establish a time line, and then we will have a clue where to begin," concludes Danny.

"Speed up a little, Danny!"

"We're running hot right now. Lights and siren. You know the rules."

"Danny, it's just different when it's someone you love."

"I know, Pete. I'm so sorry. We'll find them. Let's just get back to basics. We're here."

They both race to the back door as Pete frantically enters the alarm code.

Pete concludes, "They're in the car."

Danny interjects, "Check the calendar, and see if it tells us where they might have been today."

ROSIE REDMOND ROSEMAN

Rosie rests on the dirty floor as the minutes ticking into hours have softened her determination not to succumb to her weariness and give in to the filth.

Connie has obtained a second wind and has replaced Rosie in her role of pacing, but only briefly as her leg aches all the way to her knee.

Connie stops in front of one of the two areas that seem to have been used as a work bench of sorts. She thinks if they could find some implement they might be able to dig around the only place that seems to have air flow and gain their freedom. She locates a feeble piece of metal but quickly discards it as useless.

Yes, useless because even if they get outside, she is not even sure she would know what direction to go that would take them to the car. But then, then it hits her, and she screams, "I know!! I know, I do it at the mall all the time!"

Rosie leaps to her feet, believing Connie has broken under the strain of the moment as she blabbers about shopping.

"Connie, snap out of it. It's okay. Someone will find us."

"I know. I know exactly what to do, Rosie and, someone WILL find us!"

"Okay, what? What are you going to do?"

Connie with her gaze fixed on Rosie pulls her keys from her pocket and hits the panic button which notifies OnStar.

DETECTIVE DANIEL DOBBINS

Danny does a 360 in the middle of the Kilpatrick toll road and races back to the Hefner exit as he is told the location the emergency vehicles had been sent is on Britton Road west toward 81 Highway.

Pete's heart races as he feels the knot in his stomach rise to his chest. His erratic thought process is quickly joined by his irrational fears. He can't remember a time in his life that he had such gut wrenching feelings. Every euphoric pleasure he had known with Rosie is rushing his senses and being replaced with a sense of dread. The fear of facing life without her, without Rosie, a future that he would face alone. Oh God!

Danny brings the vehicle to a screeching halt as they both run full gait toward the flashlight beams several hundred yards ahead.

Pete hollers, "Have you found anyone?"

"No, sir. We just gained entrance by using bolt cutters on the gate as the sheriff's office is unable to reach the grounds keeper. We have been informed the car is registered to Constance Sinclair."

Pete calls out, "Everyone stop, and please listen. We're looking for two women. There were two women in that vehicle, and they have to be here somewhere."

"You men check the cabins to the west, and you four take the two to the east."

Pete stops as he hears one by one report, "all clear, all clear and a final all clear."

Danny turns to one officer and requests a squad car be pulled into the area. He reaches in and switches on the cars outside speakers. In a slow and controlled voice, he gives instructions, "Everyone, please be extremely quiet." He begins, "Rosie, this is Danny. You have to find a way to tell us where you are. Do you understand? Tell us where you are. Do it now! NOW!"

Pete feels his eyes moisten as he tenses his body to stave off the trembling into which he so easily could give. *Rosie, do it. Do it. Oh please, God!* and as all hope begins to falter, someone yells, "Did you hear that?"

"What? Where?"

"Over here. I think…Yes, over here!"

The sound of footsteps beating a trail was immense. Everyone converges on the location, and as the obstruction is removed from the cellar doors, Pete runs down the steps, lifts Rosie and carries her forward. "Oh, sweetheart. Are you okay?"

Connie is helped up the steps and softly begins to weep as she sees Pete and Rosie embracing. Yes, a moment that she knows is far beyond her longing as a deep ache revisits her soul.

CANADIAN COUNTY SHERIFF'S OFFICE

Both feel shunned at being excluded as the interrogation room door shuts, leaving Danny and Pete to pace the hall.

"Ladies, I'm the lead detective for the Canadian County Sheriff's Office, Deputy TJ Bolling. This interview is being recorded verbally and visually even though you are under no physical restraint to stay and comply. I have been informed that you both have requested to return at a later date to give your statements, so I appreciate your cooperation, and I will make this as brief as possible.

We will start with you, Mrs. Sinclair. Would you state your full name?"

"Constance Louise Sinclair,"

"And you, Mrs. Roseman?"

"Rosie Roseman."

"And Mrs. Roseman, that's your full legal name?"

"No, it's Rosie Marie Roseman."

"Okay, which of you ladies was the driver of the car that was in pursuit of the black sedan?"

"I was," states Connie. "But I would like you to know that I wasn't in pursuit of anyone, and I didn't break any laws while driving."

"I see," offers Deputy Bolling. "I am using that word casually, at this moment. Let me start again. Mrs. Sinclair, you own the car, and was the driver that was following a black sedan?"

"Yes."

"Where did the pursuit, a…where did you encounter the sedan?"

"We saw it pull onto NW Highway, just west of May Avenue."

"What about the vehicle or occupant made you follow?"

Rosie leans forward and adjusts her chair slightly askew which turns her toward Connie as Rosie intertwines their pinkies. Rosie feels Connie's tension release as Rosie assumes control. "I'm the one that saw the vehicle, and I believe there is a report with your office about an intrusion into Connie's home not long ago."

"Yes, I am aware and have requested that report for review. So you felt this car was involved in the break-in?"

"Yes."

"And what makes you so positive?"

"The video from the residence's security system was enough to make me think the driver of the vehicle could be the same person."

"So you followed? Did the vehicle do anything suspicious that you noticed?"

Rosie continues, "No."

Deputy Bolling stands and leads into the question. "The vehicle entered the property where you were found under duress?"

"Yes."

Turning back their direction, he adds, "Please continue."

"We walked the property and…"

"You drove your vehicle onto the property, exited and looked around?"

Rosie feels Connie's grip tighten, but Rosie shows no evidence of such as she informs, "No, Connie's car never entered the property in any way. We left the car on the main road and walked up the entry road to the area, but no one was around, and no car could be seen."

Connie notices Rosie has omitted using the key to verify it opened the padlock and thinks, *"I'm so glad you are telling this, because I don't know how much trouble we are in for entering private property, even though we had a key to the entrance gate."*

"Then what?"

"The cabins seemed all empty, and as we turned north and east toward the back of the property, we were pushed into the cellar."

"You saw no one?"

"No."

"You heard nothing?"

"No, nothing."

"How about you Mrs. Sinclair? You saw or heard no one?"

"Yes, sir. Exactly. It was unexpected."

Deputy Bolling knows what he is hearing is not completely the truth, but since he didn't place the ladies in separate interrogation rooms, he knows he has lost the opportunity to compare their stories separately. At this point, he has no choice but to release them, but not before a stern admonishing from him. "Ladies, this department should have been contacted at your first thought that this man might be a suspect in the break in at your home. Your cavalier behavior will be overlooked this time, but it will not be tolerated in the future. Have I made myself clear?"

PETER ROSEMAN

Pete is leaning against the wall along with Danny as he asks, "How long are you staying? Who would have thought the ER would have taken as long as it did, but Connie's foot had to be looked at."

"Yes, and that gave you time to get Connie's Lexus before it was impounded and secure the deeds that were in the backseat. Where did you put them?"

"In the trunk. I certainly didn't want them in our patrol unit," Pete states.

"Danny, you can leave any time."

Danny concedes, "I'm going soon. I'll grab a few hours rest, and then I will present the murder-arson to the DA."

Pete walks Danny to the door, and they see an indication that another tomorrow has arrived. As Danny turns to leave, he gives Pete a slap on the shoulder and a squeeze which seems to be as close to a hug he can muster, but the gesture is well received on Pete's part.

Pete returns to his patrol of the hall. He knows that this could have had a totally different outcome, but he will not go there. He stops and feels the tension release, and a slight sigh escapes as he thanks God for His protection.

Pete's phone rings. He steps into an adjacent room, acknowledges the caller and answers, "See you there as soon as they tell us we can leave."

THE DRIVE *HOME*

The drive home is arduous as her ankle throbs with every bump of the car. Connie adjusts her crutches to dig for her sunglasses mysteriously lost in the recesses of her purse. The morning sun is fierce as Pete makes the turn east off HW 81 onto nine-mile blacktop which will connect them to NW Highway.

Connie sees Rosie has placed her hand over Pete's where it rests on the gear shift. The only sound is the occasional rock as it's propelled under the carriage of the car.

Connie adjusts her glasses and straightens herself to obtain a view of the red knoll where Magic had stood erect in anticipation of her return. She knows there will be no Magic, those days long past, but her determination doesn't wane. She would continue to be resilient. Isn't that what she had told Arthur? What was the word she had used? *Yes, Arthur, I'm durable and have become well-seasoned. But why then, oh Lord, am I feeling at my wit's end, a rag that has been wrung out repeatedly, over and over with only thin strands of fiber left holding it together.*

Pete pulls the car onto NW Highway for the short distance before turning up the entrance road to the estate. Rosie opens Connie's door and steps aside. Connie maneuvers her crutches and turns to see someone, but only partially.

Connie's mind struggles with the familiarity of the figure just as he bends forward into view.

Connie gasps, tears flow and quickly are joined by sobs. He lifts her out and with arms tightly around his neck and head buried in his shoulder, Connie cries, "I'll never do this to us again. Never JJ, never."

SINCLAIR ESTATE

"Pete, I want to go home. Please take me home," pleads Rosie as she reaches for a tissue and falls into the chair. "What is wrong with me? Where's all this emotion coming from?"

JJ places a sofa pillow under Connie's leg, and Connie consoles, "Oh Rosie, I just think that the realization of our mortality has been made very apparent to us both."

Pete sits on the arm of her chair and bemoans, "Plus, none of us has had any sleep. I can push through that, though, if you feel like getting our things together."

Rosie asks, "When do you have to be back to work on the murder case? I just want to go home, so I can be with you even for a couple of hours between shifts."

"I don't have to be back to work for several days, I'm good until next week. Danny is presenting the case to the DA today."

"Oh, sweetheart. I'm only thinking of myself. You're exhausted," Rosie bellows as she sniffles and the tears flow. "What is wrong with me? I'm tougher than this."

"Rosie, you and Pete, go on up, and get some sleep or head home. Your decision. You both have been more than generous with your lives to keep me safe and secure."

Connie shifts her weight and turns to locate JJ standing just out of her view and offers, "If JJ will be so kind and get me some water, I'll take another pain pill and rest here."

JJ steps forward knowing that his whole being is revealing his disbelief in what has transpired the last weeks: the happenings to which he hasn't been privy and the circumstances that have escalated to the point of endangering Rosie and Connie's lives.

Pete instructs, "In there," as he points the way for JJ and takes Rosie's hand in his.

"Rosie walks to the couch and asserts, "Please make your way up. You need to be safely in your bed before that pain pill kicks in."

Connie nods agreement, and Rosie counters, "Give me a hug in case we're gone when you awake." The hug turns into a tearful loving encounter; then with a soft pat Pete guides Rosie to the staircase.

JJ shakes Pete's hand before heading to find the kitchen. While rummaging through several cabinets to locate a glass, JJ thinks, *Does she mean it when she says, "JJ, I'll never do this to us again!" Do what, keep secrets, keep me at arm's length, leave suddenly, not to mention abruptly. Or never do this again until Charles summons?* JJ hopes Pete will be man enough to bring him into the foal of his friendship. "We'll see," JJ blurts as he exits.

CONSTANCE LOUISE SINCLAIR

Connie wakes startled, but why, she has no idea. She lies in the stark stillness as she gasps frantically for air. She feels herself drowning in an overwhelming feeling of pure terror. She holds her head as she feels her heart beat thundering. Every thread of clothing soaked from perspiration. The blackness of the room quickly engulfs her as her single-minded focus seems to be the need to save herself or someone else. Images flash through her mind. She senses the need to be deathly silent. She fights to raise herself on one elbow but is quickly knocked back as the pain forces her to hastily drop and surrender. *Where am I, what time is it, and AM I alone?*

Slowly, as her eyes become accustomed, she sees the slight image of light from the doors to the balcony. *It's my room.* She feels beside her for her phone and then reaches out to the nightstand. It must be here, but no, she knocks something to the floor with a thud.

She hears rustling from the alcove and then, "Connie, I'm here." The desk light comes on as JJ comes forward. "Are you okay? You're trembling."

"Could you hold me? Please, would you just hold me?"

JJ quickly complies as the on-again-off-again need to secure and defend Connie returns. "It's just everything you have been through. It's okay."

As he embraces her, he thinks of the dreams of his heart, yes, the silent dreams he never exposes as a verse comes to mind…

The human heart has
Hidden treasure
In secret kept,
In silence sealed;
The thoughts, the hopes,
The dreams, the pleasure,
Whose charms were
Broken if revealed.

Charlotte Bronte

Is that it? The more of himself he reveals, the more broken their relationship becomes. *Do I reveal everything at once like ripping off a bandage or…?*

The next time Connie stirs, it is with a stretch and glance out the doors to the early morning day light. JJ is asleep at the foot of the bed as she hobbles through the bathroom and seats herself on the round ottoman in the center of her closet. Her need for a shower is evident, and a glance in the full-length mirror makes her cringe. The stamina it will take to get a shower or bath will not be an easy one so in the meantime she pulls on clean lounging pants and a tee.

Connie grabs a crutch to stand, but it snags on something. She pulls it forward and gives a quick, "Oh my," as her bra is being dragged into view. She cups her hands over her nose and mouth as she tries to remember, and just as quickly, she shakes her head to dislodge her minds trappings and cries an even louder, "Oooh my!!"

"I know," JJ states, "Your clothes were tattered and dirty and remember you asked for a second pain pill. Rosie told you not to take it until you were safe in bed but you insisted."

Connie grimaces as she has to agree.

"It left you non-functional. It had to be done," JJ states as if it was an everyday occurrence.

Connie feels a wisp of tingling sweep up her back, to her neck, and an immediate flush to her face. Her mind is sifting through thoughts that are being manifested in her head.

JJ declares, "There was no other way."

Connie, with a deep breath, thinks, *it is what it is.* "I'm sure you were discreet?"

JJ answers in a stern voice as he turns, "Absolutely!"

Connie catches his reflection in the bath mirror and momentarily sees a definite smile appear.

They sit at the bar as both ravishingly devour their breakfast.

Connie asks, "It's Saturday?"

"Yes, it's Saturday," answers JJ.

Connie nods in disbelief.

JJ remembers, "I've got our phones on silent, so you might need to check your voicemail. Also, that pile of papers on the desk is from the hospital, and you are to contact your family doctor for a follow-up appointment."

Connie turns on the barstool to stand, and JJ instructs, “Stay put, I’ll get ‘em.”

Connie places her forearms on the bar to adjust herself closer as she feels something.

JJ returns and stands on the far side of the bar as Connie asks, “What is this on the back of my arm?”

JJ declares, “Wow, it’s more mud. I thought I got all of that.”

Connie, aghast at this revelation, exclaims, “You washed me!!!”

PETER ROSEMAN

"Danny, hope everything is quiet as I need a couple more days off."

"You still feeling whipped? I just came to work Friday long enough to get charges filed with the DA, and then I split. I'm rested now, but if you're not up to par, take additional time."

"No. I'm fine. My body is used to sleep deprivation. It's Rosie. When we got to Connie's early Friday morning, she suddenly fell to pieces. I first thought she was just overcome with the events as she stroked my hand most of the way to the estate. I know we have been apart only a short length of time, but I have been lonesome, so I figured she had been, too. We spent the night and moved back to the apartment Saturday."

"You left Connie alone? The Sheriff's Office hasn't located a suspect, much less got a handle on this."

"No, she's not alone, Danny. JJ's here. He hopped on a plane soon as I told him we had no contact with the girls, and he was waiting at the estate when we arrived. I must tell you, Danny, I am appreciative of him doing that. Until we were away from the estate and on the road home, it hadn't occurred to me the impact of staying out there was doing to us."

"I know you don't know him well. Neither do I, but is Rosie okay with JJ? Are there any actions that she has made you privy to that would sway your opinion one way or the other?"

"No. She had been a go-between when things were on the rocks once or twice, but most of that was before we were married, and after we were married it just seemed like JJ and Connie were in a cooling off period."

"Glad somebody is with her as she will need attention with that foot, also. You take as long as you need, Pete."

"Thanks, Danny. Rosie's better, but she doesn't miss an opportunity to be near me which doesn't bother me any. Like I said, I think we both just really missed each other. She's pretty well over the teary-eyed stuff, but now seems to have a touch of the stomach virus."

"Talk with you later, Pete."

AMANDA BORDILLON

"Sorry we have been playing phone tag, but at least your messages told us that you had located Connie and she was safe."

"Yes, it was a long flight and seemed forever before they arrived at the estate, but am rested now."

"Have you told her?"

"No, I know you are anxious, but there is so much going on, and Connie has been injured."

"Injured, how?"

"Amanda, get Doug on the phone, so I can tell this once."

ARTHUR DRISCOLL

"Matthew, so you're still here. I want to talk to you about the police wanting to question that investigator you pressured me into agreeing to hire even though we had a very capable one already. He is always in your office, but strangely disappeared. What do you know about him?"

"You were right, Arthur. He was less than dependable, so I let him go."

"So you won't mind speaking with the police later?"

"No, just tell Julie when they're expected, so she can get it on my calendar."

"Speaking of Julie," Arthur cautiously leads, "Have you authorized over-time for her the last couple of months?"

"No, why?"

"You remember the altered files the IT people were checking into?"

"Yes."

"I'm wondering if there is something you want to tell me."

"What? What are you talking about?"

"The files that were changed!"

"I don't have a clue what you're insinuating."

"Well, let me make it clear. The IT department has been looking into the IP address for the files to determine who was logged in last."

"You're not inferring it was my computer. That's impossible."

"No, you're smarter than that, but the IP address is your secretaries, and the odd part is, security shows her signed out hours in advance of the files being opened."

Matthew turns his chair aside, leans back.

Arthur discloses, "I knew it! Do you have any idea what you have done? Look around you! All of this, all of the work of our family to shape this firm and build it on their respected name with all the integrity that should suggest and you just throw it all away."

Arthur looms over Matthew with his arms on each side of Matthew's chair as he tries to make sense of the situation. "What files exactly did you get into?"

Matthew remains silent.

"I have two ways to go with this, and my first instinct is to kick your butt out of here, and let the authorities deal with you! Let you be disbarred, lose your license, lose your livelihood, or I can try and fix this before it goes any further, like I always do."

Matthew intertwines his fingers across his chest and has no response.

Arthur, with eyes narrowed, opens his mouth to let all the contempt spill forward, but is too mad to continue as he propels Matthew's chair swiftly back until it abruptly collides with the wall.

"What have you done? Tell me. I'll find out anyway, as soon as the electronic files are compared with the originals. The first things I checked were the trusts, but they appear okay. Besides, they are monitored by three different departments plus an auditor."

Matthew moves his chair to his desk, slaps his laptop shut and sneers, "Look all you want. All files have been returned to their original content as everything I needed fell in my lap, courtesy of Constance Sinclair. The minute you came in and asked me about California Title Rights, I knew I had what I needed."

"And what is that exactly, pray tell?"

"The original title to the California property was in the safety deposit box which has what I need to access the deed."

Arthur pushes, "Go on!"

"Charles was to get me title, but then his keys were lost. I sent Deidra over to verify as she has a friend at Charles' office and Charles was telling the truth. Keys were missing, and Anna told Deidra that Charles was very concerned as his bank box keys were on his key chain.

I had gathered the money to secure the title back, and Charles said he would apply for a lost key to the safety deposit drawer and get the chip he needed to get the quit claim deed to the club."

Arthur questions, "The Gun Club? How could you let this happen?"

"I don't know Arthur, but the OK gun club is ours, except Charles passed before I got the deed transferred.

Arthur interjects, "You do realize, Matthew, that you could have done an affidavit and have him sign or even file a writ."

"I know, but it didn't happen, so I altered the files to back date the entry, and now I can petition the court and get legal title. Charles said he had a scanned copy on his computer.

We were to meet the day of his fall for him to receive payment and me to transfer documents to our files."

"Why did you feel the need to sell OK without telling me? Money problems?"

A prolonged pause follows before Matthew continues, "It wasn't a sale as such. We were at the tracks, and it was a wager between his race horse and ours."

"Gambling, again. Oh, Matthew, you couldn't just pay?"

"Charles said he couldn't wager cash, so it was property."

"What did Charles place for collateral?"

"His California oil site."

"Matthew, you need to tell me right now everything that could be revealed as nefarious on your part."

"Okay, Arthur. I thought it would be simple just to get the flash drive that Charles' killer had used to hi-jack all of Charles files, and then I'd have my document. But after several attempts, the flash could not be found, but we were able to get a couple of the document coins.

Then I heard from Deidra that her friend, Anna Miller at Charles' office said his keys had been located, so I knew it would be only time until they discovered and checked the bank box. I then could use the document which I had to petition the court and get clear title.

Next, you bring in the titles Connie has with no quit claim deeds, so now I'm back to needing either the flash drive, coin or deed."

Arthur walks to the end of Matthew's desk and states, "I think you either cut your losses and give up on this and pray we are not all implicated or we…"

"We what, Arthur?"

"We ask Connie to help locate the deeds. It will be of benefit to both of us. She needs deeds for California property, and you will get the OK deed. We interface your need with hers. You told me when you looked at the Cali title, there have to be deeds somewhere. I checked LA County Courthouse, and the last deed is the one Connie has.

If Charles had them, it's on those devices, and she is the only one that can find them."

"Well, Kirby tried."

Arthur immediately recoils with, "Kirby is out, gone and not to be mentioned again. We will do this legally from now on. I will contact Mrs. Sinclair and advise her of our need and also tell her under the circumstances, she will need to seek new counsel.

Now, let me see your court motions and writ on OK property."

CONSTANCE LOUISE SINCLAIR

"Rosie, what's wrong with you? Are you still crying? I won't keep you, but…"

"No, I'm not crying just threw up, AGAIN! Thought I had the twenty-four hour virus, but guess not."

"I won't keep you then, but have you had a chance to fill Pete in?"

"No."

"I'm wondering what the consequences of all this is. The key and everything, plus you thinking he's employed at the law firm as a bodyguard?"

"I know, we'll talk later."

"Oh, and I want to thank you for handling the interview."

"You're welcome. Love you, girl!"

"Love you right back."

Pete, with a make believe bristle in his voice criticizes, "Who you 'loving' too?"

"Silly, it was just Connie calling to check on us."

JEREMIAH JASON PAIGE

"We better get a move on. What time is your doctor's appointment?"

"Not until this afternoon, and it will take every minute of that to get this pulled together," Connie sighs as she gestures to her deteriorating appearance only compounded by the last couple of lazy days. Connie lets her mind wander as she thinks, *"Yes, these days have been nice having someone."*

JJ defends, "I know and…" just as he thinks silence might be appropriate.

Connie quickly responds as she prompts, "And what? Go on," while wishing she could put her hand on her hip, but the crutches bring an end to that thought.

JJ offers, "And nothing. Just…And what do we need to do to remedy this situation?"

"I guess I follow the instructions on the dismissal sheet. Trash bag, tape and something to sit on."

The decision to take the truck instead of the car is the right one. Even having to figure out the running boards is better than getting in the low-sitting car.

JJ turns east onto NW Highway toward Oklahoma City without any instruction and admits, "I can get us to the city, but you will have to take over from there."

"Okay," Connie confesses. "I had to look it up myself as he has moved out of Mercy's Doctor's

Tower to somewhere on 122nd. But for now, just straight to the toll road."

Connie reaches over and lowers the radio so she can talk. It's time to tell it all but where to start. She remains silent as she searches for not only words, but the right words.

JJ looks out the window at the fields of wheat making a stand even in the midst of the drought.

Connie begins to comment on the beauty of the grain in the Oklahoma wind, but doesn't.

JJ is the first to speak as he asks, "Connie?" in a questioning voice and then states, "I'm sorry," but quickly follows with, "Yes, Connie, I'm sorry, again." Then with voice escalating he adds, "No, I'm not, as I'm the only one that ever says, I'm sorry. I don't think 'I'm sorry' is in your vocabulary!"

Connie continues to look out her window, not seeing anything, just hearing the chastising words. She braces herself not to internalize any of this. No, she knew 'I'm sorry' is not something she ever has offered, not because she hasn't been sorry, but because to verbalize the statement makes her feel vulnerable, weak, even demeaned.

JJ is not even close to done as he continues, "Can you grasp the fear I felt over this whole situation? Can you grasp how many times I have let myself be pulled to you, only to be hastily dismissed? Yes, tossed away and not only myself, but Amanda and Doug, also. You seem to think that it is perfectly okay to play with peoples' emotions until you feel the need to do a slam dunk and let everyone fall where they may.

Connie, I'm not good at walking on eggs, and that's what my life with you has become. I feel the need to throw my hat in the ring to test the waters before I enter yet again. You let me know what you want me to know, only when you want me to know, if ever. I'm through asking forgiveness, over and over, for my past transgressions. Either you have accepted my position in those situations, or you haven't."

Connie has nothing forthcoming. Silence reigns.

JJ pulls over, places the truck in park, releases his seat belt and unleashes, "I didn't intend this to turn into an ultimatum, but I'm afraid it has. I can't play this game any longer. No, it's not that I can't, it's that I won't. This isn't only for me, but others in our life. Others that I love and also protect. Yes, I thought you loved also, but guess I am mistaken."

Connie cringes.

"Amanda is ecstatic for you to know something. Amanda, that sweet loving child that sees no wrong in anyone, even after you walked out, not only on me, but her. That sweet child that bared her soul to you and loves you unconditionally even now and was waiting patiently to know if you were okay. She was heart sick until she found out, but you know what, Connie? I can't speak for Doug, but I can for Amanda and me, and I'm telling you. I'm telling you, no more! The next move is yours!

The line in the sand is drawn. Cross it or stand your ground!"

CONSTANCE LOUISE SINCLAIR

They have made it to the doctors with minimal verbiage to accomplish the feat.

JJ stops in front of the entrance, refuses valet assistance, helps Connie through the swinging doors, but then retreats to the still running vehicle. She watches as he drives away.

She signs in and takes a seat. Time ticks, but JJ never appears. She thinks of walking to the windows to see if she can catch a glimpse of the pickup's location, but the struggle to rise changes her mind.

She is told at check-in that she might have a wait as they have accommodated her due to her injury and visit to the ER.

She wishes that she had never touched the radio until she knew where she wanted to begin with JJ. She has had every intention of full disclosure of all events since leaving the ranch starting with LAX terminal, but JJ has taken her silence as rejection. Can she blame him? She had done everything he stated and did it again and again.

Connie does nothing to deter the frustration she feels and knows JJ is in sheer torment. Her vexation rises as she knows what she must do. This unresolved problem can't continue, but her appointment does nothing but hinder her resolve. She struggles to her feet and makes it to the window to search for their vehicle. Her search is short.

She sees JJ two aisles over, pacing the grassy area between two trees. If she knows him, and she does, he is replaying his admission non-stop in his head, obsessing over it as she sees him talking, but only to himself.

Connie glances away as she knows there are questions to be answered and words to be rehashed. She reigns in her emotions and knows they are on the verge of irreparable damage to this relationship.

She makes her way to reception and concedes, "I'm afraid I need to reschedule as I'm unable to wait any longer," but then she feels his unmistakable presence as she hears, "No, we will wait."

JJ guides her to a secluded area where one single love seat faces a small side area. As she lowers herself, he holds her arm but never removes his grasp as he lets his hand slide into hers.

Connie accepts his hand, gives a long enduring squeeze, and softly states, "Oh, J, It's my fault."

JJ quietly cups Connie's face as he gently places her head on his shoulder.

PETER ROSEMAN

"Danny, I need another day. I'm taking Rosie to Urgent Care."

JEREMIAH JASON PAIGE

JJ slowly moves forward as they take their place in line at Walgreens. Connie is thankful they are in the truck with no console as she is snug against JJ, and he has his hand on her leg. She feels his warmth as he moves his hand in a continuous circle.

Connie has started her discourse several times, and each time JJ has silenced her. Once again, she starts, and as in every previous attempt, she begins with an apology. "JJ, I profusely apologize. I'm so sorry. I'm not worth your continued support and love. You have every right to wash your hands of me."

She feels her stomach quiver, chest knot and throat tighten as the words reverberate within her. The thought is frightening, bringing her to know she can't live with that outcome. Is he to be her forever and always?

An intense desire arises as she throws away any inhibitions she has previously let overwhelm her. She turns toward him as she feels the sheer exhilaration burst forth.

JJ sees the gleam and sparkle in her eyes as Connie declares, "You're mine. Yes, you're mine, and I claim you with every molecule of my very being. I can't imagine life without you or what I would do if you had given up on me. Please tell me you will never give up, because I don't break a promise and I, Constance Louise Sinclair, promise you, Jeremiah Jason Paige my forever and always.

The resulting kiss lasts well into the horns of the impatient drivers demanding movement of the line.

Right now a moment of time
Is fleeting by!
Capture its reality…
Become that moment.

Paul Cezanne

ARTHUR DRISCOLL

"Mrs. Sinclair, I'm calling to advise you that Driscoll and Driscoll will be unable to continue representing you or Sinclair Oil in any past or future legal obligations. It has come to my attention that your husband and my brother, Matthew, were in the last phase of completing a transaction in which a piece of real estate was to be transferred to Matthew.

A letter regarding this conversation will follow so that you may be able to seek new counsel and transfer of pertinent documents and files may be expedited."

DOUGLAS HARTLEY

"JJ, is this a good time? We are anxious to hear about Connie's doctor's appointment. It was earlier today, right?"

"Yes, Doug, this is a perfect time. Is Amanda with you?"

"Yes, I'm here," comes the answer as Amanda's light and airy personality dances into the room.

"Let me get Connie. Okay, we're here."

"Hello, you two. So happy to hear you. Everything okay out your way?" asked Connie.

"Yes, everything is great. Just missing family," quips Amanda.

"Awe, you are so sweet. You are going to bring me to tears, sweet child."

"Oh, Connie, no," implores Amanda.

"Yes, Amanda. I need to apologize from the deepest recesses of my heart for the behavior I exhibited while with you and Doug. It was inexcusable. I've apologized to J, and we have come to terms with my bad behavior."

Doug offers, "No apology necessary, all forgiven and forgotten. Besides, we just called about your doctor's visit. Hope you got a good report."

"Oh, thank you all for embracing me after my misdeeds, and yes, got a good report. He gave me some anti-inflammatory and told me to continue on the pain meds, as needed. I possibly might be in a walking boot in a few weeks which will make a monumental difference on the stairs."

Doug declares, "That's wonderful. You sound in good spirits. We are just so thankful you are okay and on the mend."

"My complete sentiments exactly, Doug. What have you two been up to? Had many races and our boy still strutting his stuff, leaving everyone in his dust?"

"Yes, he has."

"I thought so as I can hear it in your voice. There is nothing like a win to keep us motivated," discloses Connie.

"You can say that again, as the wins in my life keep coming. Amanda and I have something to tell you."

"Okay, you unquestionably have my attention."

Doug questions, "Amanda, you want to do this?"

Amanda declines, "No, you."

Connie reaches for JJ as he places his arm around her.

They both hear the release of breath as Doug blurts, "I've asked Amanda to share my crazy life and to become my wife."

"How exciting! I'm so happy for you both! What a joyous time in your young lives. You couldn't be more perfect for each other. I see nothing but blue skies and smooth sailing for you. Congrats, congrats, and congrats! I love you both."

Connie turns to JJ and asks, "How about you, JJ?"

"I must confess I already knew and Amanda was pushing me to tell you, but..." JJ's mind regresses to his and Connie's prior circumstances and quickly continues with, "...but this couldn't have turned out better and I say, welcome, Doug."

"Thanks, JJ."

Connie asks, "How'd you do it? On one knee in the moonlight, over a candlelight dinner or..."

Amanda contradicts, "You could never guess in a million years. We have babies, Amanda. Five in all, three fillies and two colts and one of the colts has captured my heart. He could be Magic's foul, just perfect. I had been working with him to get him halter broke but he just wasn't quite there. I came to the stables one morning, as usual, and there he was by his mother. They were in the paddock, and he had his halter on. I ran to see and praise him, and something was tied with a bright red ribbon. It was my ring, Connie. It was my ring tied to Beauty's halter. I quickly turned as I heard Miguel, Jose, and Felipe, cheering, clapping and whistling. I must admit I flushed at being discovered and then they parted, and he's there, Doug's there, and he blew me a kiss as he came and untied my ring. Then he tells me, 'If your face is an indication of your answer, may I place this on your finger?'"

There is silence from all, because Amanda's sweet voice has softly brought each of them to an aah moment.

JJ sighs, "I hope you two are hugging, because we are."

CONSTANCE LOUISE SINCLAIR

The rain falls quietly as it has for the last several days. Yes, the drought has been broken according to David Payne, News 9, but quakes continue in Grant, Major and Garfield Counties with the last week seeing several in Edmond, much to the residents' dismay, as the majority of the populace is the very news anchors relaying the information.

Connie watches as the furniture on the lanai receives God's rain and thinks of the leisurely drives she and Charles would take on the back roads into El Reno, just because she enjoyed the drive in a gentle rain, a rain that brings cleansing and a newness to all it touches.

JJ sees her at the window and encompasses her in his entirety. Connie is grateful for the walking boot and use of a scooter which allows her the freedom to enjoy this loving moment.

JJ wonders, "You seem deep in thought. A penny for each one?"

Do I tell him I am in the car with Charles with hands entwined while the gentle droplets encase us in the moment? Our drive to El Reno and Sid's. No Charles, you can't be erased, and you shan't, for you are just as monumental in my life now as you ever were. I feel you coming to me less and less, but you will never be replaced, because I am who I am because of you, and that's neither good nor bad. No Charles, it's a moment in our life. But the question still to be answered is, can you release me to finish my journey on this earth? Yes, this journey with JJ. Time will tell!"

Connie leans into him, yes into the arms that fits not only her current need, but seems to bring her a feeling of safety more each time and with each encounter and confides, "I wish you had been down earlier."

"Why? You should have hollered."

"Yes, I should have. It was like a fairy tale, the mist over the meadow just hung in mid-air. The birds even flew lower to be in the magic of it all."

Connie takes a deep breath and reminisces, "But my only thought right now is that you smell as clean as the rain and you've shaved."

"You don't smell too bad, either. Seems I have more time as you need my help less and less since you've gotten your new ride here."

Could she really be enjoying happiness again? Has she obtained what Rosie and Pete so freely and shamelessly flaunt with their open displays of affection?

"You're crying. What have I said?"

"Nothing, you have said nothing, but only brought me happy tears as I feel amazing and blessed. You push me. No JJ, you pull me. Whatever, push or pull, it is where I need to be, and that is here in your arms. Promise me we can stay like this?"

He lifts her up on the counter as they become lost in this moment of love.

ROSIE REDMOND ROSEMAN

"Hello, honey. How are you? Still in much pain?"

"Hey, Rosie. I'm well, and the pain is gone. Only the annoyance of this boot, but it comes off, I hope, Thursday. What have you been up to? I miss you, but I must admit JJ is a nice distraction."

"I'll bet, but it certainly was comforting to be home and in my bed and having time with my 'nice distraction'."

"Oh, I'm excited that we get to see each other this weekend."

"That's news to me," states Rosie.

"Yes, Pete and JJ spoke, and we're going out together as couples. Like double dating in high school. That is, if you feel up to it. You better after your visit to Urgent Care? I wasn't trying to hog all the attention with my minor foot injury."

The friends share a laugh, and then Rosie continues, "This might be awkward, because you need to know that the case has been given to the Criminal Investigations Department. Pete believes that Matthew Driscoll has been nothing but cooperative, and the firm's investigator that he had fired the day of our encounter is Kirby Kerman. He is ex-military. He has a brother still in, and his father is retired from Department of Justice but seems to be still working for them in some aspect or another.

"No, I didn't know, so thanks for the heads up. I spoke with Arthur Driscoll and also received a letter stating they no longer represent the company or me."

"Really?"

"Yes, seems that Matthew and Charles were in the final stages of some type of real estate transaction."

Rosie perks at this bit of incite and adds, "That might be what Joyce Chapman was saying Phillip was talking about. I'd tread lightly and carefully to be sure your interest is first priority as Driscoll denies any culpability. Pete told me that's a high dollar attorney word for 'he takes no blame' in all this. Pete says CID has the security tape from Becky's and Pete gave them your tape. They are working in conjunction with LA Sheriff's Office. And Connie."

"Yes?"

"I'm with that attorney on that culpability thing, because I'm denying knowing anything to Pete."

"What have you told him?"

"It's not that I haven't told him. It's just that the opportunity never seems right as he was, and is, so concerned about my health issue, and I don't feel up to putting everything we did on the table and having to defend our actions. Connie, I'm not physically and emotionally able to continue down that road. Can you understand that?"

"Rosie, whatever. You have always been the strong one and helped to keep my emotions in check, so I can, at this time, be strong for you.

Whatever you want is where my allegiance is, but I don't know for how long it can last."

"Why?"

"JJ knows everything. That was my promise to him: my full disclosure of my life as I have agreed we are in this together. No more keeping him at arm's length. I fear it will be only time until he and Pete compare notes."

JEREMIAH JASON PAIGE

"You about ready? We're to pick them up in an hour."

"Almost. It won't take that long to get to the city."

"I am hoping to have enough time to run the car through the carwash before we get them," states JJ.

"Good idea. It needs to be detailed, but the carwash will suffice. Could you come up, please? You're going to have to zip me and help with my necklace. I'm so happy to be rid of that disgusting boot, but sandals are the best I can manage until my foot gets stronger."

She turns as JJ walks in the room, and he lets out a whistle that covers it all.

"Thank you, kind sir. That means the world to me right now as I have felt less than attractive with my only accessories being a big blue high-top and a bright red scooter."

"Happy to oblige," he offers as he kisses the nape of her neck and smells the perfume that he never tires of.

The car is self-propelled through the wash, and in the brief moments of darkness, Connie grasps the instance to comment, "I think Rosie is in need of a relaxing evening, and she's hoping to keep the conversation off Pete's work. I assured her that conversation wouldn't be instigated by either of us."

JJ in a calm voice, queries, "Is there something I should be made aware of, Connie!"

"Yes, yes. I was trying to be discreet for Rosie's sake. Rosie hasn't told Pete everything."

"Everything, like what?"

"Pete still thinks it's just about the intruder, and he knows nothing about Phillip's disclosure about Matthew. He's not aware of us obtaining the tape from Enid, much less how we obtained it and much more."

The car is pushed forward into the light as JJ criticizes, "Are there other things I'm unaware of?" His look is piercing.

Connie places her hand on his and declares, "No, you know everything."

JJ feels Connie's inner tremor.

The ensuing drive is filled with information on how to maneuver the downtown area after picking them up. Connie directs, "Rosie and I can sit in the back and Pete can sit here as he will be good at directions, because The Vast is just a couple of blocks from the police department.

JJ smirks, "I have no problem in letting Pete drive. He's driven this car before, hasn't he?"

"Yes."

"Okay, I will sit with you in the back. This is a date, right?"

"Yes, it is. So that's settled," assures Connie. "You have to realize, JJ, I'm finding it difficult from making no decisions with Charles to having to learn to handle situations alone, and now I don't have to again, as I have you. J, I like the feeling that brings when I say, I have you!"

"Connie, can we just relax? You know when I told you, you never take responsibility for your actions and admit you're sorry? Well, you have completely done the opposite as you say I'm sorry all the time. Oh, sweetheart, you are forgiven. You need no longer to apologize, just to continue to be open and forthcoming where we are concerned. I fear where I was walking on eggs, I have made you feel the same way, and that was not my intention. Please be yourself, free of any inhibitions, free to smile, laugh and just let us have fun. Fun together. Okay?"

"I love you, J, and I once again, claim you as mine."

Connie is right as Pete deftly gets them through construction and safely to the Devon Tower front entrance. The short walk was an adventure through imported wall tiles, large fossils in stone from centuries back and a black marble infinity pool that was quite deceiving.

They enter the elevator and are propelled, non-stop, 49 floors, and then they see the view of not only Oklahoma City, but many cities, only possible from this spectacular building. They take their time before being seated in the lounge area to await their table. JJ has a bourbon and coke, Pete a gin and tonic, Connie a margarita and then Rosie slowly expounds, "Water with lemon, please."

Connie feels Rosie's discomfort and consoles, "We'll do this another time when your stomach is better."

They are shown to their table, and they all laugh as they each in turn order the No Name Ranch Steak, with the smaller cut being the only difference for the ladies.

Connie is the first to speak as the conversation unfolds. "JJ and I received some exciting news this week."

Rosie coaxes, "Really, what?" as her interest is peaked.

"The kids called from California to ask about my doctor's appointment, but it was quickly evident from their voices that something was afoot."

After a slight pause as Connie beams, she states, "Doug has proposed to Amanda and get this, in a very romantic way, at least for cowboys. He had her ring tied to her pony's halter with a red ribbon."

"How exceptional. When is the wedding?"

"Early spring, but a location hasn't been decided yet."

"Oh Connie, I know you love doing weddings, because ours was beyond anything I could have hoped for," Rosie decrees as Pete reaches for her hand.

"Rosie continues, "JJ, it was just magical. The estate had baskets of flowers suspended every five feet on both sides of the entrance road. There were valets to park all the guests' cars. The grand staircase had English ivy garland with hydrangea and roses all the way to the first landing. Under the stained glass window was an immense floral arrangement matching the garland. Caterers were everywhere with canapés and drinks. As you exited the gallery onto the terrace, the kitchen area to the north was being used to prepare all the smoked meats for the dinner to follow.

The guests were seated in white satin covered chairs, and each chair bordering the center aisle had white toile with ivy tendrils, roses, and hydrangea. The canopy covered arbor was alight in white twinkle lights and flower covered toile. Past the arbor were white tents placed in the gardens where the toasts were made, and reception dinner served.

Later in the evening, the inner tent was opened where the orchestra and dancing began. Pete and I danced, and JJ, it was just magical. I will always remember that dance and the look between the two of us, the look I pray will never end between us from then to now and forever."

Rosie begins to weep. Pete shifts to her side as he feels the need to comfort her.

He consoles, "It's okay. We can get through this."

Connie looks to JJ as she finds this most disturbing and is afraid of what's to come.

Rosie covers her face as she tries to evade the words about to be offered.

Pete chides, "This is a joyous occasion, isn't it, sweetheart?"

"Yes, yes, it is. Please forgive me," Rosie claims as she straightens to regain her composure.

Pete pats her hand and advises, "We would like to announce that we are to become parents."

Connie inhales as she realizes she has been holding her breath in fearful anticipation. "That's wonderful. We are so happy for you, aren't we, JJ? No wonder you have been in such a state. Everything makes sense now. When, do you know when?"

Rosie sniffles and beams, "Yes, early spring!"

Connie agrees, "See, two blessings, Doug and Amanda's wedding and your sweet child's birth! Thank you, Lord!"

"Connie, you have to pray for us. You have to pray for a healthy pregnancy and…"

"And what, Rosie. What are you not telling us?"

"Pete has RH factor, and I have a blood disorder called Factor V Leiden which causes blood clots. Pete hadn't told me about the Rh factor, and I had never related Leiden to him until we were at the doctors for the results of my test. Neither of us ever dreamed I was pregnant. We were both overcome to the point of speechlessness and that's when I thought to tell the doctor about my family's blood condition. I knew it was hereditary on my mother's side but nothing more. That's when Pete asks about RH Factor, and Dr. Roberts said he had knowledge on RH but was limited on Leiden, and he would research it. He then said he strongly suggested we consider amniocentesis. The full extent of the combination won't be known until later when amniotic fluid can be drawn."

Connie admits, "Oh my. That is a lot to absorb, especially going in thinking you have a stomach virus. I thought you might have picked up something from sitting on the cold cellar floor for all those hours. In the meantime, we are choosing hope and accepting this baby as a blessing from God. I will pray for…"

Rosie pleads, "Connie, do it. Pray now, please, Connie. I need to hear the words lifted to God for our child."

Connie concedes, "Of course. I've prayed in many a public place at a friend's request, so why not in a restaurant as we share a meal?"

They clasp hands, all four friends in a complete circle that encompass the child within as Connie prays, "Heavenly Father, our God, we come before you now Lord, asking for strength for Rosie and Pete throughout the coming weeks until the determining test can be done. Father, let them realize that you are always with them, and Lord, thank you that they have, not only you, but each other to sustain them. We pray for this baby, and thank you for what you are doing even at this moment. Lord, we love you, believe in your healing powers and give you all the glory and praise. In Jesus' name. Amen!"

They begin to look up, but Rosie squeezes Connie's hand and adds, "Thank you, Lord, for the love and support of friends. Amen."

Connie smiles as she returns the squeeze and each in unison say, "Amen!!"

The thought never occurs to Connie to see if anyone is aware of the happenings at their table. She gives JJ's hand a quick rub with her thumb when she sees it. JJ's distant look makes his overall appearance hard to read. *Where is he in all this? Is this too much for him? Is the thought of a child in his mind? Surely he remembers I'm incapable of children. What a terrible word to bring to mind. Incapable…I'll go no further,* Connie thinks. *No more*, but it's impossible as her thoughts come one after another, appearing as large crushing waves for only a second before being replaced with a more unsettling one.

The ladies decline dessert, but each takes a to-go of Banana Cheesecake. They walk the outer glass wall of windows back through the bar on their way to the elevator. Connie spots a crystal sculpture at the end of the room encircled in lights, and everyone agrees it is a perfect picture moment. How nice it feels to be in a couple's picture and be a part of a couple. Connie knows this picture will be framed and displayed, if only for Rosie as a pre-baby moment.

Connie and Rosie wait at the entrance while JJ and Pete locate the valet for the car. Connie comments on the multi-colored building on the right down the street. "Downtown has so much to offer, and what a beautiful night to spend down here."

Rosie is lost in thought. Connie proclaims, "Rosie, I know you are concerned, as well you should be, and the waiting can't be easy. Whatever I can do, please tell me. I can take you to doctor's appointments or even for lab work. I know, I can send someone to clean. And food. I can do food. I just need to be a help to you, to be a part of this in some meaningful way. You and Pete have bent over backwards for me. Please tell me you will call at even a hint of need."

Rosie smiles and nods throughout the conversation with a few awes and "how sweet" interjected during pauses.

"I can't imagine going through this without you. My heart is in turmoil with the what-ifs. Connie, I need you to keep me anchored and tell me the things that only you can say, like the time you have told me I'm wrong when I was making personal decisions, and I was thinking with my heart and not my head as you put it, 'trying to save everyone, instead of letting them take responsibility. That's what I want and need from you, to shake me out of negative thoughts and pull me to the positive because you are the most positive person I know. All you've been through and you're still standing and thanking God for it all. I need that. I need you to help me sustain my faith."

"Oh Rosie, we all live under God's grace, and your faith and mine both can't falter, at least at the same time. That is one thing we are good at. When I'm down, you are up, and when you're down, I'm up, and so it will be the same throughout your pregnancy, and we will continue on together, my friend. I love you."

"I love you, too."

The guys arrive, and JJ is driving as Pete opens the back door for Rosie and the front door for Connie, but Connie slides in beside Rosie leaving Pete awkwardly standing before she makes it clear she is seated by pulling the door closed.

The girls are arm entwined and continue in conversation. JJ misses no opportunity at every stop light to check the rear view for any indication of conversation, but sees only smiles and hand pats. What could they possibly be talking about so intently? This is beyond his comprehension as his male friendships have all been with hands in pockets, a piece of straw in his mouth and an occasional kick of a dirt clod.

Pete looks out the side window and only comments when a directional turn is indicated.

At their apartment, Pete and Rosie extend an invitation for coffee, but Connie declines as JJ has not made an effort to exit the car. Pete says bye to JJ and closes Connie's door as they exchange waves and drive away.

Connie instructs, "Turn here, babe, and a few more blocks down Walker and make a right on Sheridan. We can get on 40 just past Mc Donald's a couple of blocks. I think two more lights to Sheridan."

Connie turns somewhat and places both her hands on JJ's as it rests on the gear shift. "Are you okay? You were unusually quiet the last part of the evening."

Connie's fear of being shut out is unfounded as JJ unloads, "What a burden their marriage is enduring. All the circumstances of the intruder, staying at the estate for weeks on end, the stress of Pete's job dealing with the worst of humanities, the pent up fear of not knowing if his wife is dead or alive while she is being held captive, and now an unexpected pregnancy that might end badly. All of this and probably more we are unaware of in the first year of their lives together. Just doesn't seem fair."

"Slow down, or you'll miss the turn to the Interstate. It's a little hard to see. Okay, now we're good until Kilpatrick North."

Connie tries to formulate her thoughts but just as quickly as they bubble to the surface, they burst. *Why is it so easy to be in mindless conversation with Rosie? Is it because I know that she and I have absolutely been forged by fire, and nothing said between us can make our friendship falter? What was it Rosie said, something about stuck like glue? Oh, Rosie, you do keep things light-hearted.*

Connie turns her attention to JJ. "J, I know you're upset or at least having misgivings. You know life throws curves at everyone. But that's what makes it life. You just hang on through thick and thin, no matter how thin, thin gets. Forever and always. That is where Pete and Rosie are now. You heard her so dramatically portray every step of their wedding only to get to the one significant part, a very definite part that she was reiterating with Pete."

JJ looks her way and frowns, "What part? I must have missed it."

"No, you didn't. The part where they danced, as they looked into each other's eyes and they felt as if no one else was in the room. The look of love, JJ. Rosie said she never wanted to lose that feeling between them for now and forever more. Rosie was telling Pete to hang on that their life together is worth everything they are encountering and more.

Are we good, JJ? Are we to that point where we are that good?"

"I don't know. We have been through things with the results being either my fault or yours, and each one of us have come to that realization in time to rein in our relationship, to save it for another day. We are well on that road, Connie. Don't you think?"

Connie admits, "Yes, I do. We've got this."

His smile and sideward glance melts her heart.

CONSTANCE LOUISE SINCLAIR

Connie uses Charles' key from his key chain to open his office door but this time in broad daylight and not under the cover of darkness. She proceeds to the picture hanging above Charles' credenza and places pressure on the right corner of the frame and the picture begins to rise revealing the safe.

JJ questions, "What do I do?"

"I'm not certain as Rosie had to climb on the credenza. Seems as if she just ran the coin across the top. Yes, it's the very center of the top edge where it released and opened. Try there."

True to her instructions, the moment JJ places the coin, it releases.

Connie advises, "Let's close the blinds and secure the door as I want some time to look through all this. I'm glad we're early for the attorney's appointment," as she empties the contents and hands to JJ to place on Charles' desk.

JJ notices, "These are bearer bonds. I don't even know if these are redeemable."

Connie hands two bundles of cash in various denominations each banded from the bank. The last she removes are the deeds as she states, "This is what I want to take with us to the new law firm, along with the two abstracts I brought from home that were in the bank vault. Arthur Driscoll had said that these need to be moved from the joint trust to a single trust."

Connie opens the briefcase containing the abstracts, and JJ sees the California title made out to Jessie Sinclair. He takes a step back and says, "Connie, we need to take a moment to talk."

"Let's talk in the car, and don't you think it will be okay just to leave the bonds and cash here? There's a safe at the estate, and I had originally thought to move it there, but I hate to be carrying all this in public, don't you agree?"

She looks to JJ and immediately knows he isn't going to give his opinion as he has his back to her.

"J, what is it?"

JJ looks at the title with Jessie Sinclair's name and states, "I was detained at the LA Sheriff's Office about the home invasion at the ranch. They questioned me regarding ownership of Bordillon ranch and insinuated Amanda wasn't the true and correct owner and whether either of us should be in possession of the land." JJ stops without divulging Jessie Sinclair was mentioned.

"That can't be, JJ. The accountants, when I was going through verification of assets, said that Charles had moved money from Oklahoma to California to sustain the ranch, even to the point of putting the estate in jeopardy. There should be no question as to ownership. Besides, our appointment today with Flagg and Flagg will put all that to rest, I'm sure."

Connie closes the valise. JJ follows as he thinks he is intentionally withholding what he desperately wants to give voice to. Yes, he is not telling Connie what needs to be said and knows that this is exactly what he had challenged her over when he said, "The line in the sand is drawn. Cross it or stand your ground!"

FLAGG and FLAGG LAW FIRM

JJ holds the door for Connie as a buzzer announces their entry. No receptionist is apparent, only a cozy sitting area with three well-appointed high back chairs. The firm's heritage is tastefully presented with various memorabilia of days past.

Connie slows and thinks this is the complete opposite from Founder's Towers' glass walls and chandeliers but notes her need for security and safety is being met even before the consultation has begun.

Within moments, they are greeted by Emma who shows them to a small conference area and informs, "I will tell Mr. Flagg you have arrived. Is there anything I can offer you? We have coffee, water and both diet and regular soda."

JJ answers, "Coffee for me and, you Connie…?"

"Coffee for me also, both black."

Connie glances out the window at a redbud tree just as a cardinal flutters into flight to continue his day.

Connie runs her hand over the vintage square oak table and sees a framed window which validates her feeling of the legacy that is being honored and cherished by this generation of attorneys.

"Hello, please sir, don't stand. I'm Richard Flagg, and you're…"

"I'm JJ Paige, and this is Constance Sinclair." JJ thinks he hadn't used Constance since the days, years ago when he was following her.

"What can I help you with today?" He asks as he turns and retrieves a legal pad from the long narrow table holding the firm's declaration of establishment in 1901.

Connie begins, "I have been told by Arthur Driscoll that he has provided you documentation of a real estate agreement between my deceased husband and his brother, Matthew. Then I have additional documents upon which I need guidance concerning my trust."

Connie sees he has drawn a line at the top of the legal pad with an additional connecting line down the middle.

"May I see your documents?"

Connie offers the Abstract of Title along with the California title and gives him a moment to contemplate each before she continues, "Mr. Driscoll also said, that I need additional items such as a will, quit claim deed or like documents to connect any or all of these.

Richard concludes, "I would agree with that opinion. Have you had any success in that effort?"

"Yes, just recently at my husband's company, I found these in his safe." Connie presents the additional deeds.

Connie feels anxiety mounting as she catches herself intertwining pinkies with JJ much as Rosie had done to calm her in the interrogation room at the Sheriff's Office and as she and Charles did on many occasions. Connie thinks, *Please, Lord, let this be quick and easy. I'm so done...Soooo done, Lord!*

"First, let's start with the initial reason for your visit, and that's the title to the OK Gun Club. I have been told by Driscoll and Driscoll that upon your failure to transfer title back to them after appropriate compensation, they are prepared to let the courts decide the legitimacy of the sale."

Connie questions, "And your opinion is?"

"My advice, as your legal counsel, is to decline their offer at this time as the oil rights alone and location of land to current oil basins could pay you a significant amount of money under the right lease agreement."

"Mr. Flagg, I don't want the land. It almost cost my friend and me dearly just having possession of it now. If it belongs to Driscoll, then let him have it, so I might be released from any further fear, not only for myself, but for those I hold dear."

JJ asks, "The deed is to land and mineral rights?"

"Yes, the documents I have, show that a wager of oil rights in California against land and oil rights in Oklahoma were placed upon the outcome of a race between each parties horses."

Connie exclaims, "That's my boy."

Mr. Flagg continues, "If you do return the real estate, which is a kind gesture, I would try and negotiate for the mineral rights. Would you be opposed to that?"

"Well, no."

"The Oklahoma Abstract just needs to remove Charles and to be transferred to you as sole

Trustee. For the California title, I need some additional information."

"Like what?" asks Connie.

"I need to ascertain who Jessie Sinclair and Ruth Sinclair are. As you can see, this deed is from Jessie to Ruth."

"Jessie is a grand or great to Charles, and Ruth is Charles' mother."

"Now that that has been determined this can be handled in the same way as the Oklahoma property. I believe a search of court records will reveal a will from Charles' mother to Charles and that being said to you as Charles' widow."

Connie takes a relieved breath and further acknowledges her new found comfort by a squeeze to JJ's pinkie.

JJ begins to imagine what this means. Connie, not Amanda, owns the ranch. JJ moves his hand from Connie's grasp, without realizing it.

Connie's anxiety returns.

JJ feels the need to shake his head vigorously to bring back his ability to see a positive outcome to this situation.

His funds are minimal as he sold everything to rescue Connie from annihilation at the asset sale, but was too late. Later, he had the opportunity for part ownership in Magic which he purchased and gave to Connie as amends for what he labeled past transgressions.

But now, now, how am I going to save Amanda? The ranch is the only home she has ever known. His mind starts to battle, Amanda or Connie.

CONSTANCE LOUISE SINCLAIR

Connie's decision to ignore JJ's tentative removal of his hand is met with unnatural silence in the car on the ride from the El Reno law firm. She looks out the side window as the all too familiar standoff begins. Connie starts to laugh and then snicker.

This gets no response from JJ. Connie slightly stiffens her posture and gives a ho-hum exhale and criticizes, "I thought we were going to stop for a burger!" Still no reply.

Connie asks, "Could you pull over and let me drive?"

"Excuse me!" replies JJ.

Connie, to make her point, quickly hastens, "Yes, if I were driving, instead of you, I could pull over and have your attention, as you did to me not so very long ago."

"I'm hoping your silence is you taking an opportunity to carefully gather your thoughts," Connie declares with an emphasis on carefully.

"Okay, what do you want from me? What do you want to hear?"

Connie's quick retort deflects his questions decisively, making her point as she adds, "You're right. At this moment, your silence is more becoming."

At the estate, the slamming of car doors only accentuates and exacerbates circumstances.

Connie follows him into the house and unleashes, "If this is a temper tantrum, I can guarantee you, you will lose because I can throw a tantrum with the best of them. I can hold my own, tit for tat.

Connie grabs a dish and rushes toward JJ and presses, "Here, break this. Throw a real fit."

JJ turns, and Connie sees the flash in his eyes as he slurs, "Good, go ahead. You just go for it!"

"If you want to see crazy, I can show you crazy," as the dish shatters against the fireplace with the full force of her wrath.

JJ glints, through gritted teeth, "You think you hold all the cards. You think you are in the driver's seat in this relationship. Just tell me what to do, and I will bow and scrape to your every want and need. No, you can't, because Charles is still in control!!"

Connie shudders as she feels herself shut down.

Connie walks to the shattered pieces, bends and gradually collects each slowly, carefully and oh so gently, as if she is the fragments last hope for survival, and hers.

The stillness of the moment lets his words echo leaving the awareness of his true feelings he has so powerfully stated. *Is JJ right? He can't be. No, Charles has done nothing but guide me through this whole debacle. No, JJ's wrong!*

Connie thinks, *Have I made him feel degraded, worthless, used? Have I challenged his masculinity or has it been a memory, the memory of Charles?*

Connie stands with the last remnants tenderly encompassed and argues, "I was so hoping our talk in the car on the way home from the Vast could be a reality for us instead of continual hostilities and challenges."

JJ looks her way questioningly.

"Yes, JJ, when you asked about how Rosie and Pete could handle all the troubles they are facing, and I told you Rosie and Pete know that life throws curves, but that's what makes it life. Through thick and thin, no matter how thin, thin gets, they have pledged their forever and always. JJ, I asked you, then, are we good, are we to the point we are that good and you said you didn't know.

JJ takes a step her direction.

Connie backs and counters, "Well, now is your chance as it is my turn to draw the line in the sand."

JEREMIAH JASON PAIGE

JJ slumps on the sofa, his hair falls in his eyes. Thoughts of self-loathing and a wish to recapture errant words only add to the pain. The overwhelming need to retreat, yes withdraw from the situation, brood inward. He feels a pain to the back of his throat which he recognizes and identifies as the need to escape to a place of familiarity, the exact feeling Connie had when she fled home from California. How quickly the table has turned!

But what can I do? He feels resentment taking charge of his emotions. The advantage in this relationship is all Charles'. *How long must I fight something that you can't touch, hold or own? Are you wanting to be congratulated? Do you think Connie is still yours, and I don't deserve her? Well, Charles, that point I will concede!*

JJ walks the room. Doubts begin to recede, only to have his love for Amanda appear. *Connie or Amanda? Connie or Amanda? How can I choose?*

He turns, and yet turns again as the hopelessness continues to reveal itself.

No, it's Connie. Amanda has Doug.

JJ places his hand over his mouth and exhales. *Oh, Lord, everyone has this love thing figured out but me. Doug and Amanda, Rosie and Pete, and yet, I'm confused and bewildered. But, I can't live without Connie, I can't. I have to assure her of my loyalty, commitment and undying love. I know that Charles will never leave Connie unattended and will always look to her well-being, but I have the advantage, and I deserve her, and she should be mine. Oh, Lord, guide the way!*

JJ turns to find Connie as he knows he has to be the man that she wants and needs, and if that means sharing, then so be it.

CONSTANCE LOUISE SINCLAIR

Connie has found solace in the garden on their bench, yes, the bench where she and Charles often sat.

So, Charles, the truth has been stated. JJ feels intimidated. You know you will always be a part of my life, and I know that even now you still are taking care of me, and I love and thank you for that, but JJ sees and feels only the unfairness and injustice to him. I will never let you go as you are in my heart forever, my first love, and I thank the Lord for the blessing of letting me be in your life.

A firefly flashes his code to his mate, and Connie chuckles, because she knows even the fireflies are in agreement.

Connie continues, *Oh, Lord, how did I get here? Through all the seasons of my life, do I accept one more, and is it right? God, I once again give it to you. Show me the way! If JJ and I aren't meant to be together then, please show me. Make it clear, Father.*

Connie, as always, feels the peace of God after she gives everything to Him and she ends, "Thank you, Lord. All praise and glory to you."

JJ tentatively approaches and asks, "Connie, do you mind if I sit?"

Connie looks up and slowly exhales and thinks, *Okay, God, I'm ready, it's all yours. Help us find our way if it is your will.*

She moves slightly and offers, "Yes, please join me."

JJ sits on the straight back bench next to her and looks ahead at the view.

Connie continues, “It’s not the most comfortable bench, but it does have the best view of the gardens. For so long now, this has been a lonely bench, as I believe it has always been meant for two people, but only two people that are committed to each other. Two people that haven’t quickly jumped into a relationship that will only bring tears and sorrow. For you see, this bench deserves better than that. This bench deserves the pleasure of our touch, closeness and our appreciation of being in this moment with it and all the moments to come. Always putting others’ needs and desires first and embracing our surroundings by committing to a real relationship. I ask you again, Mr. Jeremiah Jason Paige, have you decided? Are we good?”

Frustrations are revealed, and the fear of the unknown is brought out in the open. The words begin to flow but flow in the direction of a new life and an equal partnership. For Connie and JJ have come to understand that when they include the Lord, their journey will be stable and secure, yes their journey through life’s moments of love.

Please join us in the continuation of this love story in the third book of the series, "Sweet Summer Rain." I can't wait to see where JJ and Connie take us. I'm not certain, as I haven't received my invitation, but a wedding or possibly two may be happening. Hugs!

About the Author

Carol Nichols

Separated by death from her husband, Glen, Carol finds herself in "A DIFFERENT SEASON" of her life as she turns to writing in May 2016.

Glen visits her often, and during the writing of her books, whole sections have been re-written at his bidding. His presence is mentioned in each book at the exact time he is with her, and as such she considers Glen co-author. (I love you, baby.)

It's no coincidence she writes murder, mystery, romance as she and Glen were both in law enforcement. She has been face to face with cold-blooded killers while transcribing their words.

Carol's legal career began her senior year as a secretary for an El Reno Law firm. She worked for the Canadian County Sheriff's Office under four different administrations and finished her Oklahoma career with the District Attorney's Office.

In southern Illinois, she worked for a prominent defense attorney. Upon their move to Pennsylvania, she continued journaling and wrote short stories.

Carol strives in her "Seasons" series to add light-hearted moments throughout and to give each book a freshness of character the reader can embrace.

Carol loves to write in one genre for a select group of people, but most importantly she writes for herself. She says, "When your mind is engaged with writing you feel less of the world's sting."

Carol adds, "I feel secure in this season of my life, and I pray this security continues in all the seasons that follow.

The third in Carol's "Seasons" series, SWEET SUMMER RAIN is due to be published in the Fall of 2018.

Made in the USA
Lexington, KY
04 November 2019

56506470R00232